COLLINSVILLE
HIGH

Books in the Forever Friends series

COLLINSVILLE HIGH

Lynn Craig

THOMAS NELSON PUBLISHERS
Nashville • Atlanta • London • Vancouver

Copyright © 1994 by Jan L. Dargatz

Published in Nashville, Tennessee, by Thomas Nelson, Inc., Publishers, and distributed in Canada by Word Communications, Ltd., Richmond, British Columbia.

The Bible version used in this publication is THE NEW KING JAMES VERSION. Copyright © 1979, 1980, 1982, Thomas Nelson, Inc., Publishers.

Library of Congress Cataloging-in-Publication Data

Craig, Lynn.
    Collinsville High / Lynn Craig.
        p.   cm. — (Forever friends series : bk. 4)
    Summary: Katelyn tells her diary about her busy fall semester, including being elected to student council, deciding to keep God and prayer in the Forever Friends club, and realizing that she and her pal Jon are becoming more than just friends.
    ISBN 0-8407-9242-5 (pbk.)
    [1. Clubs—Fiction.   2. High schools—Fiction.
3. Schools—Fiction.   4. Christian life—Fiction.
5. Interpersonal relations—Fiction.   6. Diaries—Fiction.]   I. Title.   II. Series: Craig, Lynn. Forever friends series : bk. 4.
PZ7.C84426Co   1994
[Fic]—dc20
                                                    94-7022
                                                       CIP
                                                        AC

Printed in the United States of America.
1 2 3 4 5 6 — 99 98 97 96 95 94

To

Rachel and Abigail Eisley

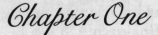

Chapter One

Starting with a Bang

I am sooooo tired, dear Journal. (I thought about putting a hundred "o's" in "so" to really make my point, but then I figured that was probably overkill.) That's why I've been so negligent in writing, I guess.

School started twelve days ago, counting the weekend, and I don't feel as if I've had a moment to breathe, until now. I've taken off Saturday from working just to curl up in my wonderful room and write, and maybe after I finish writing a little, I'll read or take a nap. Nothing could make me happier than to have a lazy day like this. I think Aunt Beverly knew I needed a rest from working in the shop. I worked lots and lots of days this last summer and had planned to work every Saturday this fall, but Aunt Beverly and I agreed last night that I should take off at least one Saturday a month, so this is it!

1

The big old maple tree outside my window is already starting to turn; a few branches here and there have lots of "half and half" leaves—half green and half a rich orange-red. I can tell this tree is going to be just glorious when it is in full "fall bloom." The tree has branches that come all the way next to the house so when I sit at my little desk by the window, I feel as if I'm in my own private treehouse. I can still see the sidewalk and the street below through the limbs, and even the houses across the street, but I have this wonderful feeling that nobody can see me. I remember when Kiersten was a little girl and she used to love to play peek-a-boo with me. She'd cover her eyes with her hands and be one hundred percent convinced that I couldn't see her. That's a little the way I feel when I look out my window through what I've come to call "my" tree.

I love autumn. Last night, we actually had to turn on the heat in the house. Grandpa Stone and Dad made sure it was in good working order just last weekend—none too soon! They also had a load of wood brought in and stacked next to the house. I'm hoping we can have a fire in the fireplace this weekend. I think I'll dig out my flannel pajamas later today.

Today is pretty cool, even though the sun is out. It's one of those days with bright blue skies, but it's just cool enough to let you know that it's *not* a summer day. Early this morning, I definitely needed to put on slippers before I went out to put a letter in the mailbox for the mail carrier to pick up. (It was a birthday card to my cousin, Kensey. She has a birthday just two days after mine so we always exchange cards.)

Autumn is my favorite time of year. The smells, the colors of the leaves, the events . . . including my birthday, of course, which is tomorrow! I'm fifteen and a sophomore at Collinsville High. Hard to believe.

And that's really what I should probably be telling you about. But where to begin? Since school started, I've been on a roller coaster that didn't seem to stop!

Starting in again at Collinsville High has been easy in lots of ways. Even though it was hard to start school here last spring, with just a few weeks left in the year, I'm glad now that we moved when we did. At least I knew my way around the school from day one this year, and I saw lots of people that I could call by name even though I hadn't seen them all summer. Of course it has been great to be able to see Jon and Trish and Kimber and Libby and all the other FF Club members in the halls and at the Snack Shack for lunch. It's pretty neat to think that I have a whole circle of friends now . . . and I don't have to eat by myself.

In other ways, it has been a rough beginning to the year. My schedule had to be changed around a little from what I had planned last spring. I still have all the classes I wanted, just not at the same times. My day goes like this: Algebra I during first period, History for second period, and Honors English for third period. Then lunch. After lunch, I have Biology, French, Physical Education, and Dramatic Arts. It's a full load! Nearly everybody I know has at least one study hour period, but I decided to jump in with both feet and take drama instead. I'm really looking forward to that course. Still, it's drama and Honors English that threw my schedule for a loop. Because of those classes, I have to take sophomore History during second period. Everybody else I know seems to have history together, and then a regular English class—in fact, the whole FF Club except Dennis and Linda have those two classes together. In all, Kimber and Trish have four classes together! They're both taking Spanish instead of French. Libby is also in their Spanish class. Just about everybody except Libby is taking geometry this year. Libby and I are taking algebra class—since we transferred in last spring and the places we came from only offered what was called a "pre-algebra" course for freshmen. Jon and Julio are both in my biology class. (Which is good. I'm glad a science brain like Jon is in my class!) Other than that, none of the FF Club kids are in my classes. I feel a little left out at times, especially when they start talking about things that happened in their classes or about people in their classes that I don't know yet.

I've also felt swallowed up with homework—even the first two weeks of school. I keep thinking, *Surely this will get better.* But if the year starts out with such a bang, will it ever get slower? Things usually start out slow and get faster! Honors English is going to be a good class and I'm really looking forward to it, but there's lots and lots of reading to do. Also a major paper to write. We're supposed to write a short story or a one-act play this fall. I think I'm going to try to write a play. I've already been thinking about ideas. In fact, I could hardly get to sleep on Tuesday night because ideas kept popping into my head.

Biology and algebra and history and French all have homework every night—something to read, problems to solve, words to learn. It's never-ending. And then there's drama. Not only do I have homework—we've already read *Romeo and Juliet* (the entire play, which I really loved, but Shakespeare isn't the easiest thing in the world to read!)—but next week, we start having after-school sessions to learn how to build a set. We're actually going to be building the set for the fall play, *The Unsinkable Molly Brown*. It's a neat story. I haven't read the play yet, but I loved the movie—one of those oldies but goodies. I may try out for a part. We'll see, as Gramma Weber says.

So, dear Journal, the days have been pretty much nonstop school and homework, Saturday at The Wonderful Life Shop and Sunday at church in the morning and youth group in the afternoon. Plus two really big things . . .

First, I've decided to run for a class office. It really wasn't my idea—at least not entirely. We were sitting around at the Snack Shack on the second or third day of school—I can't quite remember, they all seemed to run together that first week—and Jon read the announcement that had been put out about class elections. Apparently, the main student government officers are elected each spring—it must have been just before I got to Collinsville High last year—but the "class" officers are elected each fall. I guess they want to see who is actually enrolled. Anyway . . . we started joking around about who should run for office. The guys started talking about Jon running for president or vice-president, but he said he thought he'd be too busy. He's going to join the Computer Club this fall and is planning to work at Stone's Hardware two days a week after school. I think he's also considering going out for the golf team and they have a fall schedule of tournaments. Anyway, that's when everybody started talking about my running for a class office. Actually, I was in line to get my lunch when the conversation started. As I got back to our table, Libby said, "It's all d-d-decided, Katelyn."

"What's decided?" I asked.

"Our next FF Club project," said Kimber, but I could tell by the half-smile on her face that she wasn't really telling me the truth. She can't lie—not even a little bit—without giving herself away.

"Which is?" I asked.

"Getting you elected to a class office," said Trish, very bubbly. Trish has always had an outgoing personality, but in the last couple of weeks, she seems perpetually happy. I'm sure it has something to do with her obvious growing relationship with Ford . . . and also her renewed relationship with God.

"Oh, really?" I asked. I thought they were just joking. "Jon declines so I'm next in line, is that the way it is?"

"Not exactly," said Trish. "We just hadn't gotten to you yet. We ought to have at least one candidate from the FF Club."

"Well, why not you, Trish?" I asked. "After all, I'm pretty busy with the FF Club itself."

"No way," she said. "I'm a big chicken when it comes time for those campaign speeches in front of the whole class."

"You, tongue-tied?" teased Julio. "I'd like to see that."

"No, it's true," argued Trish. "I can talk to people I know, like you guys, but get up in front of a group of people I don't know? Not for a second."

I looked at Kimber with my "And what's your excuse?" look. She quickly said, "I'm new here."

"We're *all* new here," I said. "I'm just about as new as you are. If you want old-timers, you should talk to one of the guys—Ford, or Julio, or Dennis."

"No way," said Dennis. "I'm going out for basketball."

"Not me," said Julio. "I'm not into student government."

Ford said, "I'd rather help somebody else make posters."

"We'd be great campaigners for you," Trish said. "Just leave it up to us. All you have to do is look cute, smile a lot, and come up with a great speech."

"It'll be fun," said Kimber. And before I could say much, Jon was filling out the nomination form. "What office do you want, Katelyn?" he asked with his usual Jon Weaver grin. "President?"

"Heavens, no," I said.

"Vice-president?" chimed in Julio.

"No. That's almost as bad as president."

"Secretary, then?" asked Kimber.

"Well . . ." I felt really hesitant. It was neat that everybody thought I should run, and that they were eager to campaign for me, but in a way, I felt embarrassed. "Are you sure one of you doesn't want to run instead? I wish you would."

"Nope," said Libby. "You're our c-c-candidate!"

"Well, I don't want to be treasurer," I said. "Keeping track of all that bookkeeping is not for me. And class historian sounds like one giant scrapbook."

"Secretary, then," said Jon, making a big bold X in the box on the nomination form.

"When are these elections, anyway?" I asked.

"Two weeks from Friday," said Trish, looking over Jon's shoulder. "That's plenty of time."

And then the bell rang to signal the end of the lunch hour.

I walked to biology class with Jon and Julio,

who teased me all the way about being a campus big-shot once I was elected. It didn't really hit me until French class what was happening. By the end of the day I was in a panic.

Jon was waiting to walk home with me, as we usually do on Wednesdays and Thursdays—it must have been one of those days that we had this talk.

"Did you turn in that nomination form?" I asked him first thing.

"Yep," he said. "Just did."

"Is it too late to go back and get it?" I asked.

"Why?" Jon asked.

"Because I'm not sure this is a good idea. I feel embarrassed and uptight, and I haven't even done anything yet."

"And you don't have to," Jon said. "Trish and I have named ourselves the co-managers of your campaign. We've decided that we're going to have an emergency meeting of the FF Club to figure out a strategy. Ford has already said he'd work on the posters. Libby is going to try to think of some slogans tonight—you know how good she is at one-liners. And Kimber said she'd talk to Dennis about what other campaigns have been like at Collinsville High. They said something about maybe doing some handouts. It's all organized."

"And you're the one who tried to tell me this summer that organization wasn't your strength?" I teased.

"Well, it's not," said Jon, still grinning. "That's why Trish is the *co*-manager of this campaign."

"But do you really think I should do this?" I asked.

"You told me one time that you were in student government back in Eagle Point, right?" said Jon.

"Well, yes," I had to admit. "But that was a student council. Six people from each class were elected, and they weren't exactly elected to offices. Just six people each from sixth, seventh, eighth, and ninth grades were voted onto the student council. The kids on the council then elected officers. And there were only three officers: president, vice-president, and secretary-treasurer. I wasn't an officer, just on the council."

"But you were on the council all four years, right?" said Jon.

"Three of the four," I said. "I didn't run when I was in eighth grade. That was my first year in cheerleading and I knew it was going to take a lot of time."

"Still, you have lots of experience in student government," said Jon. "And you enjoyed it, right?"

"Yes," I had to admit again. "It was fun."

"Well, then," said Jon. "I think it's an excellent idea for our group to have somebody in student government. Your election will be good for all of us, Katelyn—and for the FF Club."

"Well, that might be true," I had to admit yet one more time.

"Absolutely," said Jon. "It'll give the club a much higher profile."

I didn't say anything for a little bit.

"OK?" Jon finally asked.

"Yes, I guess so," I said. "I'm still not one hundred percent convinced, but if you and the others think I should do this—and if it will help the club—then I'll run."

"Good," said Jon. "No backing out now. . . ." He made that last statement with half a question mark in his voice.

"No, I'll do it," I said.

"Good," Jon said with a grin. "I wasn't sure how I was going to ask for that nomination form back since I spent so much time telling the secretary in the principal's office what a great sophomore class officer you'll be."

"Thanks a lot," I teased. We walked on for a little way.

"Is something else wrong?" Jon asked, breaking the silence.

"I'm not sure it's a good idea to discuss my campaign at an FF Club meeting," I said. "That's sort of mixing things up a bit, don't you think? School is school, and the club is the club."

"I guess so," said Jon. "In that case, I'll just call a meeting of friends, not a club meeting." He grinned and added, "Same people, just a different title."

"I think it's important though," I stressed, "to keep the club separate from school."

"OK," said Jon. "No problem."

And so, on last Sunday afternoon, everybody gathered at Kimber's house to plan my campaign. It was like a "mini-party"—everybody brought either a six-pack of pop or something to munch on. I felt like an observer. Trish and Ford had really done some planning. They had figured out where to put up posters, and had even planned out colors and sizes. (Trish told me later it had been fun, and had given them a good excuse to spend some after-school time together. "I'm glad you're running," Trish whispered. "So glad to oblige," I whispered back.)

Libby and Julio had already designed some flyers for everybody else's approval. They came up with a slogan, "Katelyn Weber—Kwick with Words! Sophomore Secretary."

(Frankly, I'm not crazy about the "Kwick" word in the slogan. I've got this pet peeve about words that are deliberately misspelled just so they can go with another word. But . . . I didn't say anything. I didn't want to hurt Libby's feelings.)

Dennis brought up the idea of campaign buttons with the slogan on them—Trish said she knew of a place that did things like that cheaply. Kimber said she'd pay. (That was really sweet of her, but I reminded them that if it was my campaign, I should probably fund it! When I told Dad about my running for a class office, he had said he'd give me a fifty-dollar "contribution" check. I was really surprised—and grateful, of course. I also have plenty of money I've saved from working all summer. So, I told the group about Dad's check, and to my great surprise—and again, more than a little embarrassment, they decided they'd try to come up with "matching funds." They all dug into their pockets and emptied them out on the kitchen bar at Kimber's . . . the result was another sixty-five dollars.) Anyway . . . that should be enough to cover the cost of the flyers and posters and buttons. And then Ford said, "Hey, why not pencils with that on them—and maybe pass those out and just have a few big buttons for those on the campaign team?"

That's what we finally ended up with. And the most amazing thing is that it all seems to be happening pretty much without me. It's a lot like the time when my mom and friends back in Eagle Point planned a big party for my twelfth birthday. I think they had as much fun planning the party and getting ready for it as we had *at* the party. Only I didn't get to help plan it!

On the one hand, I'm glad that everybody is so excited about this—and so eager to create a bandwagon just for me. (That's Aunt Beverly's line—she asked me just last night, "How's it feel, kiddo, to have everybody creating a bandwagon just for you to ride?")

On the other hand, I have a few fears about this. Will it take too much time away from the FF Club? Would I be a good class secretary? What kind of speech should I give? How should I act around people when I want them to vote for me? (I didn't have to worry about that at Eagle Point. I had known all those kids all my life!) And what if I *don't* get elected? What will my friends think of me? Will it matter to them?

After all, I really don't know that many people at Collinsville High. I'm not sure I *can* get elected. Earlier this week I found out who the two people are who are running against me. One is a girl named Sandi. She's been at Collinsville High only one year—her family moved in from East Valley last year, so she's fairly new. The other girl's name is Lindsey. She grew up in Collinsville and is pretty popular. A girl named Sarah told me that Lindsey's planning to go out for class cheerleader, too. Two teams of five cheerleaders each are chosen to lead cheers for the freshman and sophomore teams. (If the competition wasn't this coming Monday, I'd encourage Trish to try for one of those spots. She'd be a great cheerleader. So would Kimber!)

Anyway, the competition is stiff. Sandi is very pretty and her boyfriend is a popular guy at school. Lindsey is somebody that just about everybody knows well. Who is Katelyn Weber?

At the FF Club meeting last Tuesday, we had a hard time sticking to the subject of a new project. Everybody wanted to talk about the campaign. We finally decided to schedule a meeting after the election so we could really get down to business. One interesting thing did happen, though—it's the second "big thing" I need to tell you about, dear Journal.

There's a possibility that the FF Club could become "an official school club." Dennis said that he'd heard from a guy named Bob that new clubs can be added to the activities of the school any time during September. I've got a meeting with Miss Kattenhorn—she's the school counselor but also the activities advisor—on Tuesday after school. It will be interesting to see what it takes for a club to be considered official, and also see what the advantages are.

Well, dear Journal, it's just about lunch time. Mrs. Miller baked bread and made a big pot of turkey and vegetable soup yesterday, and that's probably what we're going to have. In fact, I think I can smell it on the stove.

Now, if I can just get Smithsonian to move. She came wandering into my room about a half hour ago. I had moved over to the big chair next to my desk—just to have a change of position while I wrote—and Smithsonian walked in, jumped up on my lap, curled up, and was asleep even before I could say, "And what is it that *you* want, my big fat cat?" She's such a laze. (Is that a word? If not, I'd like to create it as one!) She didn't seem to mind at all that I continued to shift positions and write. She'd just find a new way to curl up next to me.

Well, there's Dad calling me to lunch. More later! I don't have a *clue* what's planned for my birthday. Nobody has said a *word*. I don't think they're planning a surprise . . . and I'm sure they haven't forgotten . . . but on the other hand, there's always a first! I think I'll drop some broad hints at lunch. Gotta run!

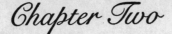

Chapter Two

One Superior Birthday!

I really don't have time to write—I still have a ton of homework to do. But . . . I just had to tell you, dear Journal, what an absolutely stupendous, fabulous, wonderful, outstanding, excellent birthday I had! It was a great day from start to finish.

Nobody gave me a hint—at all—as to what was planned for the day. I'd just about decided that it would be OK to have only a cake at dinner (except, of course, that Sunday nights at our house are pretty casual . . . we usually don't have a *real* dinnertime—we each just make our own sandwiches and maybe open a can of soup or chili. It's the one evening meal each week that Dad calls our "nonmeal meal"). Given that, a cake at *bedtime* was a real possibility!

But . . . that isn't what happened.

17

First, I was awakened at five-thirty in the morning—*way* before I had any intention of waking up—by a flashlight in my eyes, and then a blindfold was put around my head. I could hear lots of familiar voices. Somebody helped me put on my bathrobe and slippers. (I was really glad I'd worn my flannel pajamas instead of my summer ones! And I was doubly glad I'd pulled my hair up into a ponytail on top of my head. Otherwise, things could have been one major tangled disaster.)

Without letting me so much as brush my hair or brush my teeth, I was led downstairs and out the door and pushed and pulled into a car. Of course I was protesting all the way. But the more I protested, the more everybody else insisted. Finally, I just had to laugh it off. I could hear Dad's voice in the background so I knew that if all this was OK with him, there was no point in my resisting!

And off we went to the Pancake House! There, I was allowed to take off the blindfold. Sure enough, it was the entire FF gang. Guys included! How embarrassing. It would have been a lot worse if we all weren't such good friends.

"You look pretty cute when you sleep," Jon said.

"Right," I said. "A real sleeping beauty, I'm sure."

"Sleeping Beauty in d-d-disguise," said Libby.

"Hmmm. We should have found somebody to

play Prince Charming, to wake you up with a kiss," teased Julio.

"I'm sure Jon would have been pleased to volunteer," added Dennis.

At that Jon turned a little red, and I probably turned even redder. "If there had been anybody playing Prince Charming, I probably would have screamed bloody murder and we would have waked up half the neighborhood," I said. The thought of being awakened that early in the morning by a surprise kiss wasn't the least bit romantic sounding—more like a bad dream! And poor Jon. Why did Dennis have to say that? It's getting harder and harder to convince everybody that Jon and I are *just friends!*

We all ordered fruit pancakes for breakfast—the kind with lots of fruit on top and loads of whipped cream. Mrs. Miller had baked a special oversized cinnamon roll, about twelve inches in diameter. And in the circles of dough, somebody had put fifteen pink candles and one red one—which everybody said was "one to grow on."

I made a big wish—which I'll only tell you, dear Journal—and managed to come up with enough air to blow out all the candles.

The waitresses and all the other people in the Pancake House—mostly farmers and a couple of policemen—got a big laugh out of all of us, and especially me in my flannel robe and big oversized puppy slippers. (When I got these slippers last

Christmas, Scooter had a great time barking and growling at them. I think he thought two new twin dogs had arrived on his turf!)

The entire group got together and bought me a fantastic gift—a desk set for my room. It has a notepad container, a pen and pencil cannister, and a desk pad—all edged in a deep rose floral pattern. And with the set came an organizer in the same fabric. "Just what a good president needs!" said Kimber.

"And a good class secretary," added Trish.

"Not that you need help getting organized," said Jon.

"But, still. We didn't want you to mess up in planning our lives," added Julio.

I was a little overwhelmed. On top of running my entire campaign, my friends had also figured out how to get my birthday off to a really fun start.

At church, Pastor Rogers always says a special birthday prayer for those who are celebrating birthdays. He has us come forward so he can pray for the "birthday people" as a group and shake our hands. An older man, Mr. Simpson, and I were the only two who went forward. It was neat, though. Pastor Rogers prayed a beautiful prayer and it was all I could do to keep from crying.

Aunt Beverly and Grandpa Stone came to church with us, and afterward, we went to the Collinsville Club for lunch. Aunt Beverly gave me one of the neatest presents I've ever received: a stationery box. It actually looks like the top of a small roll-top desk. When you push up the roll top, there are three shelves for storing stationery. Below the roll top, there are two little drawers for pens, or things like stamps and paper clips. It's made of beautiful wood, and I know it's something I'm going to have all my life. Just right for an author. I love it!

Aunt Beverly admitted to me after lunch that she had ordered the box to sell in the shop, but the minute she unwrapped it, she knew it was meant for me. She also gave me some beautiful stationery that has a gold "K" embossed on it and gold-lined envelopes. I've never had such beautiful stationery. It made me feel very grown up.

Kiersten gave me two other boxes of stationery—one that has flowers on it and the other pale pink with an area on each notepaper that has been cut out to look like a piece of lace. Very pretty.

Grandpa Stone gave me an ink pen—the old-fashioned kind that uses real ink from a bottle. He said, "I think it's time you had a really serious pen, since I can tell that you are really serious about being a writer." He showed me tonight after supper how to fill the pen with ink and how to keep it clean. It was hard for me to write with it at first—a little, at least. The trick, I finally figured out, is not to press too hard. It's better to just let the ink flow out; I guess I thought I had to *make* it come out. I got better as I practiced a little. And I love the way my handwriting looks when I use it.

And . . . Dad gave me a beautiful gold bracelet. It's a bangle, with some etching around an area that has my initials. Simply beautiful. And also something I know I'm going to have and enjoy all my life.

I can't imagine having received any better presents. It's like they were all made just for me!

In the afternoon, Gramma Weber called, and that was really special. Dad says she's coming to our house for two weeks at Christmas this year. I can hardly wait to see her again. I really love Gramma Weber. She's very "down to earth"—or so Dad says. She has a farm—an orchard, actually—and for a while, she raised peacocks. She once told Kiersten and me that people used to use peacock feathers a lot in making hats. They were beautiful birds—big, though. I remember Kiersten scrambling for her life on more than one occasion—giggling all the way, but still running away from them as fast as her little chubby legs would carry her. Gramma Weber has a real way with words. I used to love to hear her stories about the way things were when she was a little girl. She made the stories come alive to the point where I thought I was right in them. I'm going to have to ask her to tell me some of those stories when she comes at Christmas so I can write them down.

In the evening when I walked into youth group, I saw a huge banner that said HAPPY BIRTHDAY, KATELYN! Now, that was a *big* surprise. The youth pastors, Bert, and his wife, Sharyn, had also come up with a great big sheet cake that had on it, "Here's to a fabulous fifteen."

I've never seen the youth group do anything for anybody else's birthday, but I guess several of the kids had said to Bert and Sharyn that they wanted to do something special, so they came up with this surprise. And believe me, I was surprised. Four guys in the youth group got together over the summer and practiced a lot of barbershop quartet songs. Real oldies. They've all got good voices and they came up with these neat outfits—white shirts and black pants and big red bowties. They put red garters around their shirtsleeves and slick back their hair. They look just like pictures you see of old barbershop quartets. Anyway, they're all seniors now and they call themselves the Fourth-Year Four-Parters. They're hoping, I think, to sing at parties and special events this year to make money to go to college. A pretty neat idea. The guys in the group are Dale, Tim, Mark, and Bruce.

Anyway, they sang "Happy Birthday" to me in four-part harmony and it was really neat. Then we all dug into the cake—my favorite, chocolate with semi-sweet dark chocolate icing.

Afterward, we sat around and sang songs.

There was no youth group program—just singing. Sharyn and a guy in the group named Cliff played their guitars. At the beginning of the singing, Bert said that he thought it would be a neat idea if everybody chose a song to "dedicate" to me for my birthday—and then after each dedication, the group would sing the song. Some of the songs were choruses we normally sing at youth group or in church, and some were just regular popular songs. Jon picked "You Are My Sunshine." Libby wanted the group to sing "Someone's in the Kitchen with Dinah," only change Dinah to Katelyn. It was a lot of fun. I was on the verge of crying several times, but then at another time, I laughed so hard my side hurt.

At the end of youth group, Bert suggested we all hold hands and that each person pray for the person on his or her right. When we were done praying, we were supposed to squeeze the hand of the person so that they'd know we were finished praying. He called it "squeeze-a-prayer." I'd never heard of that before. Trish prayed for me—which was very special—and I prayed for Kimber.

When I got home, I found Kiersten still up and waiting for me. She wanted to give me one more birthday hug. Sweetie!

Then Dad came into my room while I was getting ready for bed and gave me a big beautiful birthday card. He said he had decided he wanted me to read it when nobody else was around. It was a really sweet card that had a message "To My

Daughter" printed on it—about how proud the father was of his daughter and all that she meant to him. Dad had written at the bottom of the card, "I couldn't have said it better. I agree with every word of this. I love you more, however, than any card can ever say. Dad." Then I did cry. I just couldn't help it. All the good things of the day seemed to pile up into that moment. Dad hugged me and held me for a while and kissed me on the forehead.

I wish Mom could have been here for my birthday. I seem to miss her *extra* on holidays and special days. It seems as if I should be able to pick up the phone and call her and tell her all about the day. Dad said that when I feel that way, I should pray and ask the Lord Jesus to tell my mother all that has happened that is good in my life. When Dad first said that, I couldn't quite see how that would work. But when I thought about it, I realized that Mom is with the Lord in Heaven and the Lord hears all my prayers . . . so, He can pass on something from my prayers to Mom. It's made me feel better to know that Mom can know how happy I am, and yet how much I miss her and wish she could be here to share in the good times of my life. I had a good prayer time before I went to sleep.

And oh yes, I did promise to tell you my wish, dear Journal. It's something I've never ever wished before, but now seems like the right time. I wish

I might have a boyfriend this year—somebody I can really like and who will really like me back. I'm not sure if that's a prayer or a wish. Maybe it's both. Anyway . . . I did blow out all the candles!

Chapter Three

Big and Little Moments

*T*he first three days of this week have been another round of nonstop activity and homework. We had our first set-building session after school on Monday—for just a half hour, in the set shop behind the auditorium. It was neat. We saw the plans for the sets that we are going to build for *The Unsinkable Molly Brown* and they are fabulous. Very colorful. The drama teacher said that a theater major at Benton Community College designed them. (I never thought about people majoring in theater before; I guess I figured plays were just for fun, but apparently you can actually study theater and get a degree in that. That's something I just might consider—at least, I might take a course or two.)

It looks as if we are going to be sawing and hammering and painting every Monday after school for the rest of the semester. (There go Mondays! I don't know how I'm going to be able to finish my homework on Mondays. I guess I'll just have to plan ahead.)

Actually, Monday night homework is a *big* potential problem. This last Monday night's homework took me until nearly midnight to finish. Dad came in at eleven o'clock to try to get me to turn off the light, but when I explained that I still had twenty pages of English to read, he let me stay up until I finished. I normally go to bed between 9:30 and 10 P.M. on school nights, so I was really tired the next morning. And it's not as if I didn't do a little homework over the weekend. I worked about two hours on homework Saturday afternoon (which actually made it seem much less like a day off).

After school on Tuesday, I went to see Miss Kattenhorn about the idea of the FF Club becoming an official school club. She asked me about the FF Club and I told her about our projects of the summer—picking up litter along the highways and about our ride to Benton, and also about our Frisbee tournament to raise money to repaint the equipment and benches in the park. She was pretty impressed, I could tell.

I'm not sure, though, whether the FF Club should become an official school club. She had some questions about that, too. We've been charging dues for the FF Club—five dollars a month for each member. She thought that was pretty steep.

There's a limit of ten dollars a year on membership dues for a school club, and we can't keep a person out of the club just for not paying dues. On the positive side, Miss Kattenhorn pointed out that we could probably recruit lots of new members if we were a school club, and that we could keep any money we made from projects we did or events we helped to sponsor.

One of the other rules is that school clubs need to get permission from the principal before they can do projects, and especially before they can do anything that affects what Miss Kattenhorn called "the community at large." So far, we've just come up with ideas on our own, and then done them. This way seems like it might take a lot more time and effort to get something off the ground, but maybe not.

Official school clubs meet right after school so everybody has a chance to take part. I hadn't realized it before, but after Miss Kattenhorn told me about "Activity Hour," I realized that, sure enough, all the buses don't leave school right away. A couple of them wait and leave the school about six o'clock. That allows students who ride the bus to participate in sports and clubs, or to use the library. If we made the FF Club an official school club, we'd have all of our meetings right after school, and probably not more than once every month. That's the number of times most clubs meet. I'm not sure if that will work for the FF Club. It's something we'd have to consider. The meetings are set that way so everybody who wants to be a part can attend all the meetings.

Miss Kattenhorn explained that no official club can discriminate in any way against a student on the basis of race, sex, ethnic background, or year in school. That isn't a problem for the FF Club, of course. We don't discriminate either. But then she said something that could be of concern. She said, "And you can't discriminate on the basis of religion."

I said, "Well, we're all Christians in the FF Club right now. Does that make a difference?"

"No," Miss Kattenhorn said, "as long as you are willing to have people who *aren't* Christians be a part of your club. And you can't openly have a religious project or engage in religious practices or services."

"We don't have church," I said. I thought to myself about a sermon that Pastor Rogers preached this summer that we *are* the church, rather than *having* church. But I didn't say anything.

I called Kimber and Jon that night to tell them what Miss Kattenhorn had said and they were both really enthusiastic about our becoming an official school club. Kimber thought it would be a great way to make new friends at the school, and Jon thought the FF Club might triple in size overnight. I like Kimber's idea, but I'm not sure how I feel about the FF Club getting that big. I think it might be much harder to organize . . . and I can't help but wonder if we'd all still be as close.

Still, if the entire FF Club wants to do this, I guess we'll do it. We have to file the forms and have our first meeting before the end of September in order to become "official."

I think one of the main reasons for clubs to get their official status during September is so they can participate in the Homecoming Parade. Homecoming is the first football game in November. That gives clubs all of October to plan their "floats" or cars or wagons for the parade that goes from the pep-rally bonfire to the stadium. Apparently this is a really big thing at Collinsville High, and only official school clubs can be in the parade. There's a prize (fifty dollars, I think she said) for the best float, but the main reason to do your best is "bragging rights"—to say you won. I guess a good float would also help create interest in the club and more kids would join. The idea of a float sounds fun to me, but on the other hand, it all seems very much aimed at popularity. I've always thought of the FF Club as being a service club, not a popularity club. To have a float just for the sake of having a float might be fun, but what does it accomplish? On the other hand, maybe not every project of the FF Club has to accomplish something.

Anyway . . . all that will be discussed at our meeting next week, and for now, I've got too many other things to think about—like the big election speech I have to give tomorrow. All classes are dismissed tomorrow during third period. Each class is meeting in a different location; the sopho-mores are meeting in the cafeteria. All the candidates will give speeches. In addition, speeches will be given on behalf of each candidate by someone who makes the official "nomination" to the class. I had wanted Jon to nominate me, or Trish—since they are my campaign managers—but yesterday, they came up with a different idea.

There's this girl named Joannie who is in a lot of classes with Trish and Jon and the rest of the group. She was new to Collinsville High last year. (Her family moved into town from Farmer's Junction.) I remember seeing her a few times in the halls last year, but I didn't officially meet her until last week. She has started to have lunch with us, and has said that she'd like to join the FF Club at our next meeting. I like her, but I don't feel as if I know her very well.

Anyway, Trish and Joannie were talking about how many students at Collinsville High are "new"—students who have only been at the school a year or so, and who didn't go to junior high or elementary school with the "old-timers." They did an informal poll in three of their classes and they discovered that about one third of the students in each class were "new" kids. I was surprised to hear that. I guess a lot of the kids that I thought knew their way around Collinsville High last spring hadn't been there too many more months than I!

So . . . Trish and Joannie talked to Jon and they thought that I should run on a platform of representing all the new kids in the school. They said they think I should try to be the candidate who knows what it's like to be new (which, of course, I do), and that the kids who have gone to school in Collinsville all their lives could benefit by hearing some of the ideas that have worked in other places and at other schools. I thought that sounded like a good idea, although I must admit, while they were talking to me about it on the phone, I was trying to work algebra problems at the same time.

Anyway . . . they suggested that I focus my speech on the word "new" in some way, and then Trish and Jon volunteered Joannie to be the one to give my nomination speech. They said that she had won speech contests at her junior high, and last year she was a member of the Speech Club at Collinsville High. "She's a pro," said Jon, and I could tell he was really in favor of her speaking up for me. "Plus, she knows what it's like to be new, and yet now 'old' at Collinsville High. I think it's a perfect match."

"Well, if you think so," I said, "then I agree. You're the manager."

"It's not exactly as if you're a pawn," said Jon. He's big into chess. I think he and Ford have a game going pretty much all the time. One of their games took ten days! Of course, they had lots of time in between some of those moves.

I didn't say anything, but in some ways, that's exactly how I feel right now—like a pawn. I'm only going where teachers push me—mostly to homework—and to where my schedule dictates—to work, to school, to eat, to sleep, to church, or to where I have responsibilities: running for office, thinking about the FF Club. I *am* a pawn. But I certainly didn't want to admit to Jon that I'm feeling that way. He sees me as Miss Confident and In Charge.

So . . . Joannie is going to speak for me. She was very honored and excited at being asked. And . . . I've written out a speech that included two *new* ideas: a "Newcomers Club" as a way of helping new kids make friends and adjust to life at Collinsville High more quickly, and a new "Inter-School Idea Exchange," which was actually Jon's idea. Jon said he could imagine a computer network between schools (I think he called it a "bulletin board," which must be some kind of computer term) so that the kids at one school might hear about good ideas at other schools—ideas for club projects, activities, party themes, student government organization, ways to solve problems, and things like that. The Newcomers Club was the brainchild of Trish, Libby, and Kimber. They met after school Tuesday while I was talking to Miss Kattenhorn. I like both ideas—in fact, I wish I had thought of them myself!

I gave my speech this afternoon to Jon and Trish. Libby and Joannie and Dennis and Kimber were also there. They all thought it sounded good. They recommended that I change only a word or two, which I did. Joannie also gave her speech, and it really is great. I'm glad she's going to nominate me . . . I just wish we were a little better friends. We will be, I guess.

I feel pretty confident about giving the speech tomorrow. After all, it's only a three-minute talk. Joannie has to limit her speech to two minutes.

Talking in front of people has never bothered me, although I do get a little nervous. Aunt Beverly says everyone does at times, if they're honest with themselves. I gave my speech to her too—at the shop, even before I saw the rest of the group. She really liked it and gave me a couple of tips about how to pause behind the podium and smile before I started in, and how to do the same before I left the podium. I practiced several times using the counter in front of the candies and coffees as my podium. The one thing I've really got to remember is to talk s-l-o-w-l-y. I always seem to go too fast.

The only other big thing that is happening right now is something I'm trying very very hard *not* to think about. The Four Creeps—Dirk, Paul, Jim, and Skip—have started a "No Weber" campaign. Can you believe it? What nerve. They're seniors. So what business do they have worrying about a sophomore class campaign? Ford and Julio said they saw them stopping several sophomores and overheard them saying, "Don't vote for Weber, if you know what's good for you." That's awful—not to mention unfair and uncalled for!

I was ready to march right up to them and give

them a piece of my mind, but Jon reminded me that they might take a chunk out of me instead. "You really don't want to be giving a speech with a black eye, Katelyn," Jon said.

"Do you really think they'd hit me, Jon Weaver?" I asked.

"No," said Jon. "I think they'd make it look like an accident—like you ran into a wall maybe or fell down. But the result would still be a black eye. I don't want you to even think about talking to those guys. Let us guys worry about that, OK?"

"OK," I said. I was glad that Jon wanted to come to my rescue, but I was still pretty steamed. My face was probably a bit red with anger.

"Besides," Jon said, "it's probably one of those things where the less said about it, the better."

"Maybe," I said.

Oh yes, one more thing. I got a really cute card and note from Linda in today's mail. She wrote, "I hardly ever get to see you at school, but I want you to know that if I was a sophomore, I'd vote for you!" That was an encouraging word. Right when I needed it, too.

So . . . tomorrow's the big speech day! We'll see what happens!

Chapter Four

The Big Election

I got up extra early this morning so I can write a little before I go to work. The rest of the weekend seems to be booked solid so this may be the only time I have to write. But . . . the good news, dear Journal, is that I won!

I'm the new Collinsville High School class secretary!

Needless to say, the last two days have been pretty exciting. And also a bit hectic.

The speeches on Thursday weren't at all what I expected. In the first place, the audience was much more vocal than anything I ever experienced at Eagle Point! At Eagle Point, each person running just got up and said a few words and sat down. Everybody was very polite. That's not the way it is at Collinsville High! Not at all! All during a person's speech, the people in support of that person clap madly when the person makes a good point. The person's opponents might try to get a cheer going for their candidate at the same time. The result is a madhouse!

In all, there were supposed to be twelve of us giving speeches—two for president, two for vice-president, three for secretary, two for treasurer, and three for historian. Since each person only had five minutes total—three minutes for the candidate and two minutes for the nomination—that was a full hour of speeches. So, at the last minute, literally, the teacher decided that our speech time needed to be reduced to four minutes, *including* the time we took to get up to the platform. (The candidates and nominators had been allowed to leave second period fifteen minutes early, so we could meet with Mrs. Bolton, the student government faculty advisor, before the assembly. That's when Mrs. Bolton told us the new game plan.)

So . . . Joannie and I were scrambling. Actually, Joannie was in a minor panic. She just couldn't seem to figure out which part of her speech to cut out—she was using my name and saying something about each letter: W for winner, E for energetic, B for bright ideas, E for enthusiasm, and R for realistic. And she felt that she couldn't cut out more than a line or two and still have things make sense. So . . . I had to cut my speech at the last minute—almost in half. Since there was so much confusion all around—with people holding up banners and calling out cheers for their favorite candidates, I just barely got my act together before the assembly started. I felt as if I was in a zoo and some of the animals had escaped from their cages!

When the president speeches started and the hooting and hollering, too, Sandi—one of the girls who was running for class secretary—ran out of the auditorium about halfway through the second candidate's speech. The person nominating her went running after her. And that was all we saw of either of them! When time came for class secretary speeches, Sandi was no place to be found, so given the rules of the election, her name had to be withdrawn from the ballot. (Someone said later she was so nervous she thought she was going to be sick.)

During Lindsey's speech, there was some applause from her fans. The people in support of me didn't boo or anything . . . but when Joannie got up to give her speech, they all stood and started chanting, *Web-er, Web-er, Web-er*. I was already nervous. That just made me embarrassed, but also more determined, in a way, to do a good job for them. What I hadn't counted on was the appearance of The Four Creeps. Just as Joannie finished and Jon and Trish and the others stood and started to chant again, *Web-er, Web-er, Web-er* . . . The Four Creeps stood up and began to holler, "*No*

Weber, No Weber, No Weber, No Weber." Some of Lindsey's supporters joined in with them. It was a real battle of the chants!

On top of being nervous and embarrassed, now I felt mad. And most of what I had planned to say went right out the window. I probably would have stuck with my speech more if I hadn't known that Jon and Trish had made flyers to pass around that had a headline, "What You Get When You Win with Weber," and under it, a photocopy of one of the photographs Jon took of me when he was goofing around with his camera last month and a paragraph each about the Newcomers Club and the Idea Exchange. Instead of talking much about those ideas, I talked about how we needed a true sophomore class representative, not somebody that *seniors* came in and ordered us to have, and that I considered it an honor that these particular senior hecklers didn't want me elected. I guess my basic theme was "sophomores have ideas, too" and some of them are better than senior ideas. In particular, the sophomore idea of electing Katelyn Weber was better than the senior idea of not electing her. I'm not sure where all that came from, except that I was mad and Joannie had gone overtime by a few seconds and I really only had about ninety seconds to make my point. I didn't realize until later that I had talked about myself as if I was talking about someone else—very objectively!

It seemed like lots of people cheered when I

finished and The Four Creeps seemed to disappear from the room. Ford told me later that Mrs. Bolton and Mr. Scott had ushered them from the room while I was talking. As everybody exited, I went over and shook hands with Lindsey and told her she gave a good speech. Meanwhile, Trish and Jon and everybody else in the FF Club were frantically handing out flyers and saying, "Vote for Weber."

All through lunch, people kept coming up to me, telling me that I had done a great job and that they were voting for me. That gave me a lot of confidence, but I felt sure that people were also saying that to Lindsey. Trish and Jon were really psyched, and Ford was about as "up" as I've ever seen him. He just kept saying, "The woman had fire in her bones!" Ford is normally pretty laid back and quiet, but I can tell that Trish is having an influence on him. He's talking more and is a lot freer to show some emotion. (Good for Trish!) Julio kept repeating, "What a speech. What a candidate. What a woman." Finally Libby looked at him and said, "What a b-b-broken record!"

We were all pretty happy, though, at the way things had gone. It was hard to concentrate during fifth and sixth periods. I kept getting my verb conjugations all jumbled up in French class.

Thursday night, Trish and Jon organized a phone campaign. They had divided the people in the sophomore class into eight groups and each person—Trish, Jon, Libby, Julio, Dennis, Kimber,

Joannie, and Ford—took a group and called as many people as they could to say, "I hope you'll vote for Katelyn Weber for class secretary tomorrow." They didn't call Lindsey, or Sandi, or the people working on their campaigns, and we didn't have to call ourselves, so that meant that each person had about twenty-five calls to make. They didn't want me to call, so I felt a little out of it, spending the evening doing homework while everybody else was campaigning for me. I told Aunt Beverly how I was feeling and she suggested that I write each person on my campaign committee (which is basically the FF Club, plus Joannie Field, who will be a member by this time next week) a note, thanking them for their support. I did that Thursday night and I felt a lot better.

I must admit, though, I had a hard time getting to sleep on Thursday night. I kept going over the assembly in my mind, trying to figure out if I had said the right thing, or if I simply should have ignored The Four Creeps. Someday, somehow, I've got to come to grips with those guys. Maybe they'll just graduate next spring and disappear. There's an idea!

I was also a little nervous about how I should react if I win . . . or if I lose. I almost think it would be easier to lose and say, "That's life. I'm sorry we lost," than to say, "I won!" Kiersten's opinion, of course, is that if I win I should just jump up and down and yell at the top of my lungs. I think she could probably get away with that, but I know that's not me.

As it turns out, I very nearly jumped for joy in spite of myself.

The voting was all day long. Ballots were available in several places. You had to sign a student roster for your class in order to be given a ballot, just like in a national election. (I went with Dad last year when he voted for president so I saw how it's done for real.) There were three ballot boxes— one by the principal's office, one at the cafeteria exit, and one by the Snack Shack. Students could vote until the end of seventh period. And then Mrs. Bolton and several other teachers took the ballots, separated them by class, and counted them very quickly. They had the results by 4:50 P.M. Lots of kids stayed around after school to see who had won. Jason Towle is our class president. He's a neat guy and I'm sure he's going to be a good leader; I voted for him. Chad Young is vice-president. I really don't know him, but I voted for him based on his speech. Claire Davies is treasurer. She's a nice girl, but she wasn't my choice. I voted for Michelle Adams, a girl in my French class who I can tell is both smart and reliable. Thomas Fisher is historian. And Katelyn Weber is secretary!

We all did shout and jump up and down. Kimber kept saying, "Good, good, good, good, good," and we all joined her in saying that as we passed hugs all around.

I think I was just as excited for everybody else as I was for myself. More, probably. They had all worked so hard, and so much as a team, it really was *their* victory far more than mine. I was just sort of along for the ride, it seemed.

Jon told me on the way home that he felt that even The Four Creeps had helped me win. "When the other students saw who was against you—guys the rest of the class doesn't particularly like—it actually made them vote *for* you, I think."

"But, Jon," I said, "that wasn't fair to Lindsey. She didn't ask those guys to lead a campaign against me."

"No, but she didn't stop them, either," said Jon.

"What was she supposed to do?" I asked. "She had already given her speech."

"She could have stood and booed them with the rest of us," he said.

"That would have taken some pretty quick thinking on her part," I said.

"She had all evening to come up with a little flyer stating that she had nothing to do with their behavior. Quick Print is open all night. She could have plastered the school with that and probably could have won back some votes."

"I guess," I said. "But then again, she didn't have experts like you and Trish to map out her political strategy."

"No, and she didn't have anybody as good as Joannie to give her nomination speech."

"True," I said. I was a little surprised he brought

up Joannie. "At least she was chosen as a cheerleader."

When I got home, I called Dad at the hardware store. Mrs. Miller was excited, of course. Trish had already called her. And Kiersten was jumping all over the house singing, "You won, you won, you won." Doesn't anybody say anything just once anymore?

Dad apparently called Aunt Beverly because before we knew it, we were all going out to dinner together at The Barn. And by "all" I mean just about everybody! Dad, Grandpa Stone, Aunt Beverly, Kiersten, Kimber and Dennis, Jon and Mr. Clark Weaver, Ford and Trish and Mrs. Miller, and Libby and Julio. Even Linda showed up. (Joannie had something else planned, I guess.) We got a huge table and Aunt Beverly brought a big bouquet of balloons. It was a victory party!

I literally collapsed into bed, I was so exhausted . . . even though it was only nine o'clock. Such a week! Maybe now things can settle down and I can get into a routine that is a little more organized. I'm behind in an assignment for English class and I've *got* to catch up. That's not the kind of class I can afford to get behind in.

At least I woke up bright and early this morning. When I opened the shades I was surprised to realize how much the leaves have changed since this time last week. It seems that nearly all the leaves have changed, or are at least half changed.

One more week and things should be at their peak.

Gotta go. I'm looking forward to spending the day at The Wonderful Life Shop. It seems a long time since I was there, at least for more than just a few minutes.

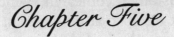

Chapter Five

Changing Seasons

Saturday
9 P.M.

I'm back again. Twice in one day. That's probably a record for my journal-writing, especially in the last few weeks. And, dear Journal, I'm not in as good a mood as I was early this morning. The most awful thing has happened. Aunt Beverly and Mr. Clark Weaver have decided to "cool it for a while." (At least, that's the way Aunt Beverly put it.)

I hit The Wonderful Life Shop this morning all bubbly and overly enthusiastic—I have a tendency to do that; it's something I'm still working on. Even though Aunt Beverly had heard all the details about the election and the victory, I felt I had to tell it all to her again. She seemed happy for me. We were both really busy, too, unpacking some boxes. My main job on Saturday morning is to dust everything—at least as much as I can before the first customer comes in, which is usually shortly after we open at ten o'clock.

It wasn't until a little before we opened that I realized that Aunt Beverly just wasn't acting her usual self. Even though she seemed excited for me, she wasn't full of hugs and questions, like she normally is.

"Is something wrong, Aunt Beverly?" I asked.

"Oh, I think I'm just a little tired this morning," she said.

"Late date?" I teased.

"Yes, it was a pretty late night," she said, but I noticed she wasn't teasing. She was serious and even a little sad.

"Did something happen?" I asked.

"Well," she began, "I'm not sure it's all that interesting, Katelyn."

"Sure it is. Everything you do is fun for me to hear about," I said. And it's true! Aunt Beverly leads an absolutely wonderful life as far as I'm concerned. She's active in lots of things and has lots of friends and travels lots of places. She's got a great shop and is busy planning to open her second store in Collinsville. And she's got a growing romance—in my opinion, of course—with Mr. Clark Weaver. What wouldn't be fun to hear?

"You'll probably find out sooner or later anyway," she said. About that time, I sensed something was really wrong.

"Like what?" I said. And wouldn't you know . . . just at that very inappropriate moment, two customers came in. And to make matters worse, they weren't coming in for anything in particular, but "just to browse." I usually love customers like that because Aunt Beverly has taught me to ask them if they are browsing for themselves or for a gift, and if they are browsing for a gift, then I get to point out things I especially like. But these two women were just browsing for themselves, and when that's the case, Aunt Beverly wants me to back off and give them plenty of shopping room. So I did. And they browsed forever! Finally, one of them bought a couple of bags of flavored coffee—Aunt Beverly had made a batch of Almond Creme coffee this morning, and it did smell heavenly. The lady bought one bag of that and one of Orange Cappuccino, which is rapidly becoming a best-seller, I think. The other lady finally bought a silver frame, two books, and a little stationery box. It seemed to take forever, though. As soon as they had closed the front door behind them, I asked again, "What am I going to find out sooner or later?"

"That Clark and I have decided to cool it for a while," she said with a sigh.

"His idea or yours?" I said.

"Mutual, I think," she said.

"What do you mean by 'cool it'?" I asked.

"Just not see each other quite so much," she said.

"But why?" I asked. "You always seem to have a lot of fun together!"

"And we probably still will," she said.

"So why?" I asked again. And in walked another customer. This one, however, knew exactly what she wanted, thank goodness. She had to buy a birthday present for her granddaughter, so she headed straight for the classic children's books and the teddy bears. She picked out one of each in not more than five minutes. (Boy, do I like customers like that!)

"Why, Aunt Beverly?" I asked. "If you have a good time together, why are you 'cooling it'?"

"Well, Katelyn . . . ," she said, and I could tell she was working to find the right words. I don't like it when she does that. It makes me feel as if I'm being given only part of the truth.

"Can't you just tell me from your heart?" I said.

She laughed and said, "Yes, I think that probably is best. The fact is, Clark and I have been spending a lot of time together lately. He's been helping me refinish the floors at the new store and put in the shelves and racks. I think we've worked at the store nearly every night for the last two weeks, scrambling to try to get everything ready so we can open in plenty of time for Christmas shopping. Some of the stock has started to come in and the sign is supposed to go up in a week or so. Colleen has quit her job and is planning to start the first of October full-time. But until then, she can only come over on Saturdays since she has some late shifts at the place where she works in Benton. So . . . it's just been nonstop."

"I know the feeling," I said.

We both sighed. In harmony. Which meant we both had to laugh.

"We're too busy," I said.

"Two women who are too busy to stop to think about being two too-busy women," Aunt Beverly said. We both laughed again.

Trying to get back to the subject, I said, "So did you have a fight about the store?"

"No, not exactly," said Aunt Beverly. "I tried to get Clark to take some money for helping me so much. I told him he had put in so many hours it was as if he had been working a part-time job, but he wouldn't hear anything of it. And I felt guilty having him work so many hours for nothing."

"Maybe he just wanted to work for fun, in order to be around you," I said.

"That's what *he* said," Aunt Beverly replied. "I truly am grateful for all his help, but I don't want him to ever think I'm using him—"

"He probably doesn't feel used," I interrupted.

"That's also what he said," Aunt Beverly replied. "But the more we talked, the more we realized how tired we both were, and how hard we had worked, and that we just didn't seem to have time lately to have *fun* together. All of our conversations have ended up being about the new store and about what needs to be done, and by when."

"What does that have to do with not seeing each other?" I asked. I was puzzled then, and frankly, dear Journal, I think I'm still puzzled now.

"The later it got, the more we both fell into this thinking that it might be nice if we just saw each other for laughs and relaxation. Like an ideal world, I guess," she said. "Clark asked me if that meant that I didn't want him to come over to the store anymore, and I found myself saying I thought that might be a good idea—I think primarily because I thought that's what *he* wanted me to say. So . . . he said 'Fine' and 'I'll call you when things get a little less frantic' and he left."

"Was he mad?" I asked.

"No, more sad," she said. "I realized after I got home that I had probably overstated everything. I was just so tired last night after we left your victory party. Clark did say, 'If you do need me, you know the number to call. I'm glad to help.' So I don't think he was angry."

But, dear Journal, I think I am . . . at least a little. Aunt Beverly should just have gone home and gone to bed after the party. I don't think Mr. Clark Weaver minded in the least working at the store. I wouldn't have minded. But I can see how he would have thought Aunt Beverly wanted him to stay away a while. The whole thing just seems like one giant communication problem to me.

And I'm also a little worried about Aunt Beverly. She still has a lot to do to get the store ready for its grand opening, which is only about two weeks away. Who's going to help her? I feel like I should volunteer. But I don't know where *I'd* find the time, and that makes me feel a little guilty.

Lots of customers came in throughout the rest of the day so I didn't have a chance to talk with Aunt Beverly further. There were still two customers in the shop when I left at five after five. Aunt Beverly told me to go on, and she'd close up on her own. I could see she was exhausted, but I did what she said. I didn't want to say anything that might make her feel even worse. I thought surely she'd be at our house for dinner tonight, but she wasn't. I told Dad about how tired Aunt Beverly was and he said that he'd noticed it too. He was thinking about volunteering to help her. He said he had volunteered a couple of weeks ago but she didn't need any help then.

"Now might be a different story," I said. I didn't tell him why I said that.

"I'll talk to her again, then," he said. That makes me feel a little better . . . at least about Aunt Beverly.

I'm still upset for her, though . . . and I can't help but wonder how Jon feels about all this. For the first time, I'm really questioning if this is something I can talk to Jon about. In the past, I've always been able to talk to Jon about everything. But romance problems between his dad and my aunt—that's something else.

So, you can see, dear Journal, that I'm a little stressed out tonight. The victory yesterday was great. But today was a bummer. And I've got tons of homework to do before Monday morning. When, oh when?

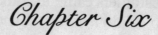

Chapter Six

Official Status

*J*ust a few quick words, dear Journal. Once again, it's a break-neck week. Monday was off to a roaring start, and we worked later than we had planned on the sets. I didn't get home until six o'clock, barely in time for dinner. Dad was a little upset that I was so late. And again I had to stay up until almost midnight to get my homework done. This is *not* a good routine as far as I'm concerned! But what to do about it is another matter.

Everybody was so nice on Monday. Lots of kids came up to congratulate me on winning the election. The results were posted several places so that those who hadn't stayed around on Friday would know the results. Our first student council meeting is Thursday after school. From what I hear, every other Thursday is a council meeting. There go Thursdays!

Yesterday after school we had an FF Club meeting. We met at our house. We got there just as Mrs. Miller was pulling two cookie sheets of oatmeal chippers out of the oven. They smelled heavenly. She had put butterscotch chips in one batch of cookies and chocolate chips in another batch. By the end of the meeting, nine of us had eaten six dozen cookies and finished off a gallon of milk! We just kept popping those cookies in, one after another.

At our meeting, we took in two new members: Joannie Field, and a guy named Smith Carlton. I just met Smith yesterday. Ford and Jon met him in their computer class the first day of school, and after they told him about the FF Club, he said he thought it sounded like a great club. They asked him if he wanted to join. He said, "Maybe." But Monday, he asked again if membership was still open in the FF Club. He told Jon, "You guys amazed me. I watched you all during Katelyn's campaign and you were really organized, but also had fun together. I'd like to be part of a club like that." So . . . he applied and we voted him in.

I met him yesterday at lunch for the first time. He normally works in the principal's office during the lunch hour—a part-time job, I guess, helping with attendance records on the school computer. He said he'd rather do it at lunch than after school, because he also has a part-time job. That sounds like a pretty full schedule to me, and maybe not a lot of time for the FF Club, but he told Jon he thought he could take part in most of our events. He seems like a really nice guy. Quiet, but with a very quick smile. You can tell he's very intelligent and isn't into every fad that passes by.

Julio and Dennis both like him, too. And I must admit, it's nice to have another guy in the club. As it is, the girls still outnumber the guys six to five. Jon said there were two other kids who were thinking about joining the FF Club, so maybe we'll have more members to take in at our next meeting.

Our main topic for discussion, of course, was whether we should be an official school club. The vote was unanimous that we should go for it. Everybody seems to think that we'll get lots of new members and that our being an official club will make us feel more a part of the school. I could tell that Kimber was just a little hesitant—one night on the phone I told her some of my fears about our becoming an official club. I'm still a little hesitant, too. But we both voted to fill out the school form which we spent about a half hour doing (while eating cookies).

We have to name an advisor for the club and Jon and Ford both recommended Miss Scaroni, their computer teacher. (Libby also has her for typing class.) Sounded like a good idea to me. I asked her today if she would be willing to be our advisor, and she said she'd be honored. She's also the advisor of the Computer Club, but she said that lots of teachers are advisors for two clubs. I guess nearly every teacher either advises a club or helps out with one of the sports teams, or something.

So this afternoon I filled out the final couple of lines on the club application and dropped it off at Miss Kattenhorn's office. I found out the deadline for filing forms is October 1, but the final approval as an official club isn't until October 15. A club has to have at least one meeting by then. We put down that our first meeting will be next Tuesday after school. That means this week is our week to get out information about the club. Jon and Ford and Trish are going to work on a little flyer about the club and Julio and Libby said they'd make a few posters about our first meeting time.

It seems more and more that "Trish and Ford" are always working on something together, and also "Libby and Julio." I've *got* to talk to Libby about this a little more. Every time I say anything about the Libby-Julio team, she just says, "He's a really nice guy, Katelyn." And I always respond, "I *know* that Libby. But what else is happening?" And she always says, "We have fun together." We've had this identical conversation three times already!

We're all assuming that we're going to be accepted as an official school club, so we went ahead and talked about what kind of float we might like to have for the Homecoming Parade.

We came up with some great ideas. Off-the-wall, awesome ideas. But the ideas were also soooo wonderful we knew that we really couldn't do them, if you know what I mean, dear Journal. Either it would take too long or too much money to make them—or we'd need special engineering. I know Dad could help in that area, but we want to do this on our own. So . . . we were a little stumped.

Finally, Joannie said, "We could always have a hay wagon as our float."

"A what?" asked Julio.

"A hay wagon. We used to go out to this farm just outside Farmer's Junction for hay rides. A tractor pulled around this wagon, of sorts, piled high with hay. And everybody would climb aboard and ride around."

"To where?" asked Dennis.

"Just around the farm," said Joannie.

"And this is f-f-fun?" asked Libby.

"I know it sounds a little dumb," said Joannie, "but hay rides can be fun. Usually somebody would bring along a guitar and we'd sing songs. And sometimes we'd stop halfway on the ride to build a campfire and tell stories and roast marshmallows. Of course we always tried to schedule the hay ride on a night with a full moon so there would be lots of light and shadows."

"A good time to tell scary stories," I said.

"Right," said Joannie. "It's all kind of old-fashioned, I admit. But still, it was fun."

"Old-fashioned fun isn't bad," said Jon. "Besides, we're sort of an old-fashioned club."

"Speak for yourself," said Dennis.

"You know what I mean," said Jon. "Our values and all . . ." He shrugged his shoulders but we all knew what he meant.

"It would be pretty cheap and easy to do," said Kimber.

"Easy to do" struck a chord with me. I had already been trying to figure out where I would find the time to build a fancy float.

"Do you think the farmer would let us rent or borrow his tractor and hay wagon?" asked Ford.

"I think it might be arranged," said Joannie. "I'll ask him."

"Do you mind?" I said.

"Not at all," she said. "He's my uncle."

"Well, in that case," said Jon. And we all laughed.

"What would we do on the float?" asked Kimber.

"Sounds like we could sing," said Trish. "Anybody play a guitar?"

I know Trish was asking that as a joke, but to her surprise—and mine—both Ford and Smith raised their hands. "You play the guitar?" asked Trish, looking at Ford in surprise. "Why didn't I know that?"

Ford smiled and said, "You never asked."

"Yeah? Well it's about time I got a serenade," said Trish.

Ford and Smith began comparing notes about what kind of guitar each of them has, and about what songs they know how to play. This just might work!

"What should our sign say?" I said. "We've got to have a sign of some kind on the side of the wagon."

Everybody was a little stumped on that one. There's not a big connection between the FF Club and a hay wagon, when you get right down to it.

"How about 'Having Fun as Friends'?" Trish finally suggested.

"And we could add 'Pulling Our Weight,'" said Jon. "Get it? The tractor pulling the wagon . . ."

"We get it," said Libby. And then the idea hit me that we could combine the two ideas!

"Why not do them both—'Pulling Our Weight and Having Fun as Friends at the Same Time!'" I said. Well, actually, I blurted it out.

"As usual, Katelyn to the rescue when we need somebody who is quick with words," said Dennis. He put a special emphasis on "quick with words" to remind everybody, I guess, of the campaign slogan.

Everybody else thought it was a good idea, too, so that's what we ended up with. Jon called me this afternoon to tell me that Joannie had called him and said that her uncle would be happy for us to borrow his tractor and hay wagon for the Homecoming Parade, and that he'd even drive the tractor for us, or teach one of the guys how to do it.

I couldn't help but think, *Why didn't Joannie*

call me? But I didn't say anything to Jon. Most of what I know about Joannie seems to come through other people. I'm going to have to try to get to know her for myself. But when? She's not in any of my classes. She isn't helping make drama sets. She isn't on student council. She doesn't work at The Wonderful Life Shop. And she doesn't go to Faith Community Fellowship. So . . . this isn't going to be very easy. Maybe we'll have a chance to get to know each other while we work on the hay wagon float.

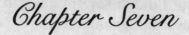

Chapter Seven

Emily's Story

Friday
7:30 P.M.

*I*t's a cold rainy night. And even though we have a fire in the fireplace and I'm curled up in front of it, it's a good night for feeling sad.

In the first place, I'm here at home and everybody else I know is at the football game. I came down with a doozy of a cold yesterday afternoon and it just got worse and worse during the day. I really wanted to go to this game—it's our first home game of the year. We beat River Bend High last week, 14 to 6. But I knew Dad would never let me go with my snuffly nose. And for that matter, he didn't even give me a chance to ask. He just wrapped a blanket around me after supper and pointed me in the direction of the fireplace and said, "In bed by nine o'clock and no excuses." He and Aunt Beverly and Grandpa Stone and Kiersten and Mari went to the game anyway. Football is a big thing in Collinsville. Football is much bigger here than in Eagle Point—or, to be more accurate, Castle Rock. Nearly everybody in town goes to the games. Except for me, of course.

I've tried to concentrate on homework, but I can't seem to focus my eyes all that well. This cold just seems to fill my entire head. In fact, I probably wouldn't even try to write except that I have a very sad story to tell you—maybe the saddest I've ever heard in all my life.

I told everybody at dinner last night—as usual, Grandpa Stone and Aunt Beverly joined us for dinner—about the FF Club idea for a hay ride. Dad and Aunt Beverly thought it was a great idea and Kiersten got very much out of sorts when she realized that only FF Club members were going to ride the wagon in the parade. Dad started telling about hay rides that he went on as a teen-ager every Halloween, and Aunt Beverly told about two hay rides she went on when she was in college.

I asked Grandpa Stone, "Did you ever go on a hay ride?"

"Yes," he said. "I did. Just one. It was lots of years ago." He seemed a little sad, but sometimes Grandpa Stone seems sad when he talks about long-ago times, especially if they were things that he did with Grandma.

"What was it like?" asked Kiersti, very eager to hear lots of details.

"Well," said Grandpa Stone, clearing his throat, "it was one of the saddest days of my life."

"Why?" asked Dad. "Did something bad happen?"

"Yes," said Grandpa Stone. "Something terrible happened." And then, seeing the looks on Kiersten's face and mine, he added quickly, "That's not to say that hay rides are bad or that something bad would happen on your hay ride, Katelyn. It's just something that happened to us back then."

"What was it, Grandpa?" I asked.

"We all drove our jalopies out to a farm that used to be where the Suncatcher Inn is located now—you know, a few miles past the city limits out in East Valley. It might have been Halloween. I don't really remember. What I do remember is that it was a night with a full moon and we were all in pretty high spirits, laughing and joking around. We made one round of the farm—it must have taken about an hour—and we were singing and cutting up."

"That doesn't sound very sad to me," said Kiersten when Grandpa Stone paused to take a sip of his hot tea.

"No, not at that point it wasn't," said Grandpa Stone. "After we had made one round, one of the guys asked the farmhand who was driving the rig—the hay wagon was pulled by a team of four horses, not a tractor—if he could drive the rig himself for a second round. The man asked him if he knew how to handle a team and he said he did—he had grown up on a farm. So the farmhand let him take over the reins."

Grandpa Stone took another sip of tea but none of us said a word, even though we were all eager for him to get on with the story.

"About halfway through that second go-round, some of the guys—maybe three or four of them— pulled out flasks of whiskey from their coat pockets and started passing them around. Granted, it was a cold night, but it wasn't *that* cold. I think they thought the party would be more fun if we all had a little whiskey in us."

I saw Kiersten get tears in her eyes. And Dad looked pretty sad, too. Just the thought of alcohol of any kind makes us all sad—we all remember the day when the police told us that if the man hadn't had that one last shot of whiskey at the bar, he probably would have been able to at least put on his brakes a little bit before he hit Mom's car broadside.

Grandpa Stone went on, "So, those two flasks began to get passed around and just about everybody was taking a swig. Including the driver of the rig. We finished going around the second time, and then started around a third time."

"Still drinking?" asked Dad.

"Yes," said Grandpa. "Some of the guys were getting pretty tanked up. And most of the gals had taken a few nips, too—all except for one gal named Emily. She wasn't about to have any whiskey and a few of the guys started teasing her about it as we went around the third time. She pulled away from them and moved toward the edge of the wagon. The more they drank, the more they tried to get her to drink. And the more she protested, the more they tried to get her to take a swig, and each time, she pulled away a little closer to the wagon's edge."

"Were you drinking, too?" asked Kiersten. I could tell she desperately wanted to hear that Grandpa Stone hadn't had any whiskey. I wanted to hear that, too.

"I'm sorry to say that I was," said Grandpa Stone. "Probably not as much as the other guys. I think I only took one or two swallows when a flask passed my way. I remember that a couple of times I put the flask to my mouth but didn't drink. I've never been that big a fan of whiskey."

Grandpa Stone paused again and got a faraway look in his eyes. We weren't sure if he was reliving the moment or trying to keep from telling the rest of the story. Maybe he was fighting back his own sadness. Aunt Beverly said, "You've got to tell us the end of the story, Mr. Stone. You can't just leave us dangling here."

I'm glad she said that. Grandpa Stone sort of "came to" when she did, and he continued, "Somewhere along the way on that third round, the guy driving the rig missed a turn. He'd probably had enough alcohol at that point that he wasn't paying close attention. Whatever the reason, we started going down a road that was much rougher than the one we had been on—it was down toward the creek that ran through that farm, and not up by the fields. There were big mud ruts everywhere, and the wagon hit a huge rut in the road just about the time Emily pulled away one last time from the guy who was trying to get her to take a drink from his flask. She was right at the edge of the wagon at that point, and when the wagon hit the rut and lurched to the side, she fell off and rolled under the wagon. The back wheel ran right over her stomach."

"Oooooh," said Kiersten closing her eyes. "She didn't die, did she, Grandpa?"

"Yes," said Grandpa, "I'm afraid she did, Kiersten."

We all groaned.

"That was back in the days before ambulances, of course," said Grandpa. "And there we were out in the middle of the night, on a road in the middle of a farm we didn't know. Another guy and I were probably the most sober of the lot. We jumped down right away and tried to help Emily, but we could tell she was hurt pretty bad. She was moaning something terrible. So, we ran in what we thought was the right direction toward the main farmhouse. As it turned out, we weren't running in exactly the right direction, but we ran far enough to see the lights of the farmhouse and then we just took off through the field toward it. They rang up the doctor and he came out as quickly as he could. We loaded Emily into the back seat of his car and I went with him to the hospital in Benton. They did emergency surgery on Emily but she had pretty severe internal bleeding and had lost so much blood that she didn't make it through the surgery."

"Grandpa, that's so sad," said Kiersten.

"It was very sad, Kiersten," said Grandpa. "Emily was one of the nicest girls in our high school. One of the prettiest, too. A real Christian girl. She went to the Baptist church where our family went. Her death was a tragedy this town didn't soon forget."

"Did anything happen to the guys who had been drinking?" Dad asked.

"No," said Grandpa Stone. "But I think we all wished that there could have been some sort of punishment for *all* of us. It might have made things a little easier, I think. As it was, one of the guys—the guy who tried to get Emily to take that drink—turned into an alcoholic. Even though it was alcohol that had caused his tragedy, it was to alcohol that he turned. He died of liver disease before he was even thirty. The rest of us pretty much swore off liquor for the rest of our lives. The good news is that a few of the guys and gals who hadn't been very regular in going to church started going again. We all grew up a lot that night."

Suddenly I put all the pieces together. "Grandpa!" I said. "Is that Emily the one who has the plaque in the park by the school?"

"Why, yes, Katelyn," Grandpa said. "Have you seen that plaque in the little garden with the fountain?"

"Of course. I went there nearly every day during lunch the first few weeks we were here in Collinsville. It was like my own little private place. I've been wondering about Emily ever since, and I have been meaning to ask you about her a dozen times at least—but I've always forgotten. I just *knew* there was a story there, but I had no idea it was such a sad one."

"Yes," said Grandpa Stone with a big sigh. "Those of us on that hay ride made that little garden for Emily and we worked and saved and put together enough money to buy that fountain and have a plaque made. We finished the garden just the week before we graduated from Collinsville High. And we dedicated the garden as part of our graduation ceremonies."

"That must have helped her family feel a little better," Dad said.

"A little, I think," said Grandpa Stone. "Still, she was their only daughter. They had two sons, but Emily was the light of their life. She had a beautiful voice and sang solos in church about once a month. It was really hard for me to forgive the guy who tried to get her to take a drink. We never talked about it, but I'm sure it must have been hard for them to forgive him, too—in fact, for them to forgive all of us."

"Were you in love with Emily?" asked Kiersten. I was about to give her a "no" answer on Grandpa's behalf—after all, Grandma Anna was Grandpa's wife—but Grandpa Stone surprised me by saying, "Yes, I think I was, Kiersten. At least a little."

"You were?" I asked, surprised, to say the least.

"Yes, a little at that stage. You see, she was my date that night. I was the one who had asked her to go on the hay ride with me."

"Oh, my," said Aunt Beverly. And then she caught herself and added, "That made it even harder for you, you poor dear." She leaned over and gave Grandpa Stone a hug.

"I felt guilty about it, no doubt about that," said Grandpa Stone. "I asked myself for a long time what would have happened if I hadn't asked her to go with us, or if I had suggested we do something else that night. I was mad at myself, of course, for not standing up to that guy who was trying to get her to take a drink. I kept thinking I should have made sure we got off at the farmhouse after we finished the second go-round of the farm. But, after a while, you have to go on. I asked God to forgive me. And I asked the Pearsons to forgive me. And then I had to forgive myself."

"I can see why you might not think a hay ride is such a good thing," I said, not sure whether my eyes were filled with tears because of my cold or because the story was so sad. Probably both.

"Oh, I don't think there's anything at all wrong with a hay ride, Katelyn," said Grandpa Stone. "The hay ride isn't what caused Emily's death."

"Grandpa's right on that one," said Dad. "Your hay ride won't be like that one."

"Just keep alcohol off the wagon," said Grandpa. "If I thought any of you were going to have liquor on board, I'd set fire to that wagon before I'd let you get on it."

"Oh, Grandpa," I said, going over to give him a hug, "I would never allow that to happen either. You know how I feel about Mom's death and about alcohol. Besides, nobody in the FF Club drinks."

"Neither did most of us who were on that hay wagon ride," said Grandpa Stone. "Until that night."

About that time, Dad realized that they were going to be late for the kick-off of the game if they didn't hurry, so he scooted Kiersten upstairs to get her coat and scarf and gloves and cap—she really does hate to bundle up. Her protest is, "All these clothes *limit* me." At Eagle Point we rarely had to wear anything more than a sweater and scarf, or a light jacket. Winter's going to be a lot colder here in Collinsville. I helped Aunt Beverly clean up the table and put away the food while she loaded the dishes into the dishwasher.

"I don't think you should let Grandpa Stone's story discourage you, Katelyn," Aunt Beverly said while we were working.

"It doesn't," I said. "It just makes me really sad. I've wanted to know Emily's story ever since we moved here—but now that I know it, I'm almost sorry that I do. It brings up a lot of other feelings that I thought I had put in the past."

"I know, honey," said Aunt Beverly, giving me

a really big hug. "Me, too. And your being sick doesn't help matters. Would you like for me to stay home with you tonight?"

"No, you go on," I said. "I'll be fine here." I wanted Aunt Beverly to have a fun night out. It was the first night in ages she hadn't been down at the new store.

"Well, I certainly don't want you to come into the shop in the morning," Aunt Beverly said.

"But I might be lots better by then," I said.

"No way," she said with a big grin. "You're not going to infect *my* good customers."

"All right," I said. Actually, I'm a little relieved I don't have to think about getting up early in the morning.

Aunt Beverly said as she hung up the kitchen towel, "Try not to think about Emily's story too much while we're gone tonight, OK?"

I nodded yes, but as you can tell, I've thought of very little else all evening. Emily's story is one of the saddest stories ever—and it's especially sad thinking Grandpa was part of it.

But, dear Journal . . . the idea just hit me—I could probably write this story as my play for Honors English! I think that's what I'll do. Maybe it will help other kids not drink! If I felt better, I'd start right now, but as it is, I can hardly breathe. I think it's time to use some nose drops and go to bed.

I probably won't get to sleep right away. It seems like every few minutes, I hear strains of the pep band playing, or the crowd yelling. This must be quite a game. I wish I knew what was happening and who was winning. I guess I'll just have to wait until later to find out.

Chapter Eight

Missing Out

Monday
8:30 P.M.

I am *not* in a good mood. Yet once again. I seem to be having a terrible time, ever since school started, feeling as if I'm on top of things, or that things are really going well.

I know you probably think I'm crazy, dear Journal, since I just won an election for sophomore class secretary, but even in that, I have a little bit of a hollow feeling—that I didn't really win, but that others won "for" me.

The summer was so neat. Every day I was busy with my friends or working at the shop, and now, I seem to be spending all of my time with my nose in a book—which isn't bad, except that these books all seem to be textbooks. I miss my friends.

Kimber called me earlier this evening to tell me about the game on Friday night—which we won, by the way, 24 to 21, with our team scoring

74

a field goal in the last two minutes of the game. She said it was the best football game she had ever attended. (That's really something for Kimber. She's not much into sports. In fact, I'm not sure she even knows the rules of football. She mainly goes, she told me one time, just to be with people. She likes the excitement, not the game.) All the kids in the FF Club sat together in the bleachers, including Joannie and Smith. And Linda and her new boyfriend, Kent. I met Kent just once, very briefly, when Linda and Kent drove by as I was getting ready to cross the street in front of the school. Kent seemed like a nice guy—but what can you really know in just a couple of minutes? Linda said she was trying to talk him into joining the FF Club.

After the game, everybody went to Tony's for pizza.

"The entire club?" I asked.

"I think so," said Kimber, and she went ahead and named everybody, "Dennis was with me, and Julio and Libby and Ford and Trish rode with us."

"Packed car," I said, "but you guys probably didn't mind, right?"

"Not really," said Kimber. "Dennis and I sat up front and I asked if someone else wanted to sit up front with us but all four of them wanted to cram into the back seat."

"Are Libby and Julio really a couple?" I asked.

"As much as Ford and Trish are, and Dennis and I," she replied.

"Has Libby talked to you about this?" I asked.

"Sure," said Kimber. "We talk about Dennis and Julio all the time. Why?"

"I just haven't talked to her that much about it," I said.

"You're so busy, Katelyn," said Kimber. "We all know that."

"I'm not *that* busy," I said.

"Well," said Kimber, "it seems like you are. You always seem to have something going, or you tell us how much you have to do. There have been a few times when I've wanted to call you but haven't because I was afraid I'd be keeping you from something important."

"I wish you'd call anyway," I said. "I'm never too busy for friends."

"I'm glad to hear you say that," Kimber said. "Tell Libby that, too, all right?"

"Do you think Libby thinks I'm too busy?" I asked.

"Maybe too tired more than too busy. She said one night when she called you, all you did was yawn on the phone. She said she felt as if you were about to keel over and fall asleep . . . and it was only nine o'clock."

"I don't remember that," I said.

"I know," said Kimber. "That's how we know you're too busy and too frazzled."

"What do you mean?" I said, truly not having a clue.

"Well, you don't remember," she laughed. "You forget—including *us* sometimes."

"Like when?" I said, feeling truly indignant. That just couldn't be the case!

"Like last Sunday when we were supposed to meet at Jon's house at two o'clock to go swimming at the Collinsville Club," she said.

"Kimberly Chan," I said, "I don't have a clue what you are talking about. I didn't know you guys were going swimming at the Collinsville Club."

"Sure you did. It was Julio's last day as lifeguard for the season. Actually, it was the last day the club was going to be open for swimming and it was still warm enough—or so we thought—so Julio asked if we could all come as his guests. You knew about that!"

"I most certainly did not," I said. "How was I supposed to know?"

"Well, we were all talking about it at Jon's on Thursday after school."

"I wasn't at Jon's on Thursday after school."

"Oh, that's right. Joannie said you had student council. She said she'd call and tell you about Sunday."

"Kimber," I said, trying to keep my voice under control, "I didn't have student council last Thursday. The first meeting is this *next* Thursday after school."

"Oh really?"

"Really. And I didn't have a clue that you were all going over to Jon's house. Who was there?"

"Well, Dennis and I, and Joannie and Julio and Libby, and Ford, and Trish."

"Kimber," I said, "Joannie never called me."

"That's weird," she said. "She said she would."

"Why didn't you say something Sunday morning at church?"

"We didn't go to church Sunday morning, don't you remember? Mom slept through her alarm and if Mom doesn't wake up, none of us seem to. So, we missed."

"Well, somebody could have called me on Sunday afternoon before you headed out."

"We probably should have," she said, "but we all thought you knew. In fact, I distinctly remember Joannie saying, 'I wonder why she isn't here. I told her two o'clock sharp.' We waited for you till almost two-thirty and then we went on. You told me at youth group that you had worked on homework all afternoon so I didn't bring it up. I figured you decided to study instead of go with us."

"Kimber," I said, "this makes me really upset. Joannie didn't call me. She knows she didn't call me. Why would she lie about it? What's going on?"

"I don't know, Katelyn," said Kimber. "I hadn't thought anything of it until now."

"So you went to the Collinsville Club and had a good time?"

"Sure," she said. "It was a blast. But it was too cold to swim for very long. The pool was warm enough but the air was pretty cold. We mostly sat in the Jacuzzi and watched Libby dive."

"Libby *dive!*"

"Yeah," said Kimber. "Julio has been teaching Libby some fancy dives, so she showed us she can do a back dive and a front flip and a swan dive. She's really good, Katelyn."

"Good grief," I said. "I am out of it. The last time I went swimming with Libby she could hardly dog paddle her way out of the deep end."

"Not anymore. She's a really good swimmer. In fact, she said the other day that Julio is trying to talk her into trying out for the swim team next spring."

"Libby?" I asked. I could hardly believe it. Four months ago, Libby didn't even want to get into a swimsuit to go to a church party. Two months ago, she could hardly swim and didn't know how to tread water. Now she's doing fancy dives and talking about the swim team. Dear Journal, I am definitely behind the times!

"Sure. She and Joannie were also trying out some water ballet moves. Joannie's a good swimmer. They even had Jon and Julio trying some of the routines with them. It was crazy, but really, they were pretty good."

"What else have I missed out on, Kimber?" I asked. I was almost afraid to find out.

"Well, we went to Burkette Farm to pick out pumpkins on Monday after school. Dennis drove us. You had drama lab."

That was true. I had been building sets until six o'clock.

"And Tuesday, Jon and Joannie and Dennis and I helped Trish rake leaves for her grandmother."

"And where was I then?"

"I don't know," Kimber said. "Isn't that the afternoon you stopped by Miss Kattenhorn's office to turn in the application so we can be an official school club?"

"Probably."

"And then you weren't at the game Friday night because you were sick," she said, her voice trailing off.

"So you went to Tony's Pizza and I missed that. Anything else?"

"Well, I called Saturday afternoon and your dad answered and said you were taking a nap and still weren't feeling too good, so you probably don't even know that we wanted to invite you to go with us to a movie."

"No, I didn't know that," I said, trying not to sound upset. "What did you see?"

"It was an oldies double feature. We saw *Wait Until Dark* and I nearly jumped out of my skin a couple of times. That's one of the most suspenseful movies I've ever seen."

"I know," I said. "I saw it on video last winter with Dad. What else?"

"A movie called *Breakfast at Tiffany's.*"

"Sounds like an Audrey Hepburn film festival," I said.

"Actually, I think it was," she said.

"Who went?" I asked.

"Ford and Trish drove over with Linda and Kent. And Jon and Joannie went with Dennis and me."

"Jon and Joannie?" I asked. Something about the way she said that made me feel as if the bottom had fallen out of my stomach. "Were they on a date?"

Kimber laughed. "Now, Katelyn. You know better than that. Jon never dates. He always says whoever he's with is 'just a friend'—same as you do."

"Did you go anywhere after the movies?"

"We got something to eat at Burger Haven and then drove back. It was pretty late. Almost eleven, I think. If it's any consolation, we dropped Joannie off at her house and then took Jon home. I barely made it home before curfew, which Dad had extended to eleven-thirty for just that one night."

I felt only a little relief.

"Anything else, Kimber? I'm feeling as if I've missed absolutely *everything*."

"Well, you missed youth group last night because you were still sick. And today you missed school, so we didn't think you'd be up to our getting together to design a sign for our float. Jon said he thought it would be a good idea if we had a sign to propose at the meeting tomorrow after school. You do remember that we have an FF Club meeting tomorrow?"

"Of course," I said. "Kimber, if you'll notice . . . I haven't forgotten anything that I *knew* about.

I've only missed the things I didn't know about or was too sick to go to!"

"I'm sorry, Katelyn," she said. "I don't think any of us really intended to leave you out. I'll make sure we don't in the future."

"So who helped make the sign this afternoon?" I asked. I wish now that I hadn't.

"Dennis was there, and so was Joannie. And Jon, of course. Didn't I say we met at his house?"

"Yes, you did," I said, and then realized that I'd only whispered my words, so I repeated them. "Yes, you did, Kimber."

"Are you all right, Katelyn?" Kimber asked.

"Yes," I said, and was glad she couldn't see my face so she wouldn't know I was lying a little. "Kimber, are you sure there isn't something between Jon and Joannie?"

"I haven't really thought about it," Kimber said. "I could ask her."

"No, don't do that," I said. "It just seems as if every time you mentioned Jon being somewhere with you guys, you mentioned Joannie being there, too."

"She's nice, Katelyn," said Kimber. "I know you don't feel as if you know her very well yet, but I'm sure you're going to like her when you do get to know her. She's a lot of fun, and she's also got a lot of good ideas."

"I'm sure she *is* nice, Kimber," I said. "I'll see you at the meeting tomorrow after school. It's in the cafeteria, right?"

"Right. See you then."

Dear Journal, I felt miserable after I hung up. I wanted to run upstairs to my room and cry and cover my head with my pillow, but Kiersten came along and asked me to help her with a math problem—she's learning to do long division right now. By the time I got up here to write, the urge to cry had passed, but I do feel very confused and very alone.

How can I get to know someone that I don't really care to get to know right now? I realize that Joannie wouldn't have any reason *not* to like Jon. After all, I've made it clear a hundred times that Jon and I are just friends. But Jon hasn't called very much lately, and when he *has* called, it's been mostly about business. Maybe he's feeling like his dad is feeling about Aunt Beverly—that it's better for our friendship to "cool it" for a while. I don't like that, and it's not at all what I want. He should at least take *my* feelings into consideration and we should talk about it. But what am I going to do? Call him and say, "Hey, what's with you and Joannie?" Frankly, I really don't want to know. I'd just die if he said, "Well, we're a couple now." Jon and I may be just friends, but I'm not thrilled at the idea he might be *more* than just friends with someone else.

Still, Kimber said he was calling Joannie "just a friend." Does that mean, though, that he considers her equal to me? Great. I've known Jon for months, and she's only known him two or three weeks and we're equal in his eyes?

I know I shouldn't start wondering like this, dear Journal, but I can't help it. All my friends still seem to have plenty of time for each other—and most of them are pairing up with boyfriends or girlfriends—and I'm the only one left out in the cold. I guess there's still Smith Carlton. He's not attached to anyone . . . at least not yet. Maybe I'd better spend some time getting to know him, rather than get to know Joannie.

It's too much to think about right now. I think I'll take the advice of Scarlett O'Hara in *Gone With the Wind*—one of my favorite novels, by the way. I just read it last winter before we moved to Collinsville. Everybody said it was too old for me, but I read it and loved it. Anyway, Scarlett's famous line is, "I'll think about it tomorrow." And that's what I'm going to have to do, too. My head is still too full of cold to have much room left over for figuring out life's problems.

Good night, dear Journal.

Chapter Nine

Questionable Status

Wednesday
9:30 P.M.

*W*e need to talk, Katelyn."

I knew immediately from the tone in Miss Kattenhorn's voice that something was wrong . . . but I didn't have a clue. She was waiting for me outside my biology class after fifth period. "Can you come see me right after school?" she asked.

"Sure, Miss Kattenhorn," I said.

I spent a lot of French and theater class thinking about what it *might* be that she wanted to talk about, but frankly, dear Journal, I couldn't come up with a thing.

Our meeting of the FF Club on Tuesday after school had been a big success. About twenty new kids showed up—several I had never seen before, and only three that I knew by name. *Jon might be right*, I thought. *We could really grow.*

Jon opened the meeting in prayer and Libby

read the minutes of our last meeting and then gave a fabulous treasurer's report. I was really proud of her. She hardly stuttered at all, and the few times she did, nobody laughed. I think if somebody had laughed, I would have voted no on joining the club! But back to the matter of money. With what we made from the Frisbee tournament on Labor Day, we have nearly $250 in our account right now. Miss Scaroni whispered to me that she thinks we just might be the richest club in the school.

We didn't have any old business, except the float, so we talked about it. Everybody liked the sign that Jon and company had made. We made our new-member recruitment campaign our "new business" and we passed out membership application forms—something Ford had whipped up at the last minute in computer class—to the new kids who were there. We voted in eight new members, kids who were ready to fill out applications right then and there. Kent was one of them, and I could tell that really made Linda happy.

Everything about the meeting was in good order. Julio closed in prayer. And we were out of the cafeteria by five-fifteen, which is the time all club meetings are supposed to be over.

Miss Scaroni complimented me afterward on what a smooth meeting it had been and how professional I had been in conducting it. She thought the idea for our float was great.

Jon walked home with me and it was just like

old times. As you might imagine, I had one eye on Jon and Joannie just about the entire meeting, trying to see if there were any sparks or secret looks between them. I didn't see anything, but then again, I really didn't want to see anything, either. Joannie looked real cute yesterday. She had her hair pulled up in a French braid and was wearing a neat sweater with pumpkins all over it. She and Jon walked in together, but I noticed that they didn't sit together. She sat down next to Trish and then Julio and Libby came in and sat next to her while Jon came up to the front to talk to me about something. That's when I asked Jon to stay and open in prayer. By the time he got back to the front row, there was no place to sit except next to Julio. Which means, in a nutshell, that their *not* sitting together didn't mean anything . . . not really.

On the way home from school, Jon was all grins and teasing. His usual self! He seemed to think that the meeting had gone really well and he was very excited about the number of new kids who were there to consider becoming members. He thinks we'll have fifty people in the FF Club before the year is over.

"You don't think that's too many?" I asked.

"No," he said, stretching out his no to have umpteen "o's." "The more the merrier, Katelyn. Just think of how much more we can do if we have lots of kids involved."

"I guess," I said. "I never imagined being president of a *big* club."

"You're great at it," he said. And he sounded sincere. More than once I wanted to bring up the subject of Joannie, but I just couldn't seem to get the words out of my mouth.

"I like the design you came up with," I said.

"I'm glad. I wish you could have been there. But really, when it comes right down to it, Kimber is such a good artist, we're all probably going to like anything she ever comes up with. There was actually no need for any of us to be there, except maybe to give her moral support and to applaud." Still no words of Joannie.

"Kimber tells me you guys went to an Audrey Hepburn Film Festival," I said.

"Well, we didn't know that's what it was when we went," Jon said. "But sure enough, that's what it was. We just thought it was a great way to see two movies for two dollars. That theater showed twelve Audrey Hepburn movies last weekend. Two on Friday night, six on Saturday, and four on Sunday. If a person saw them all, I guess he'd be an expert on her acting career."

"I probably *have* seen them all," I laughed. "She was one of my mom's favorite actresses."

"Say," Jon said, "I saw your Aunt Beverly at the game on Friday night. Why wasn't she with my dad?"

"I don't know," I said. I don't know if Jon just

wasn't saying anything or if he really doesn't know. "Do you?"

"No," Jon said. "But Dad's been home three nights this week and that's kind of unusual. He and your aunt didn't have a fight, did they?"

"I don't think so," I said. After all, "cooling it" and "having a fight" *are* two different things.

"I hope not," Jon said, and I was really glad to hear him say that.

"I know Aunt Beverly has been super busy with the new store," I said. "She hardly ever comes over to dinner. I think it will be a big relief to have the store open."

"I guess I'll see her Saturday. I agreed to go ahead and have my photograph taken so she can hang it as part of her wall decorations."

"You did? Great! What made you change your mind?"

"Oh, I was joking around with everybody a couple of weeks ago about my being a model. I thought it would make everybody laugh, but instead, everybody thought it was a great idea. They encouraged me to do it—which surprised me. But hey, if it will help out your aunt, then I might as well."

"I don't remember your joking around about that," I said.

"You weren't there. It's the day you stayed home to study while the rest of us nonstudent slugs went swimming at the Collinsville Club," Jon said.

"I didn't know you guys were going swimming, Jon," I said. "If I had known, I would have gone too."

"Really?" he said, sounding genuinely surprised. "I thought you told Joannie you couldn't go."

"I never talked to Joannie about it," I said.

"That's strange," Jon said. "I could have sworn she told me that she had talked to you and you said that if you weren't there, that meant you had to study and to go on without you."

"Nope," I said. "I never talked to her." Jon got a very puzzled look on his face.

"And," I added before he could say anything, "I *would* have gone with you if I had known. I only studied that afternoon to get a head start on the week. It wasn't as if I had a big test on Monday or any major assignment to write."

"I should have called you myself," Jon said. And dear Journal, I was *really* glad to hear him say *that*.

"Thanks," I said. "Just don't forget me next time, Mr. Jon Weaver." With a major tease and my very best French accent, I said, "I don't like to be left alone."

"Well, you've got a pretty heavy schedule this fall," Jon said. "We all understand that."

"True, Jon," I said, "but you all matter a lot to me. You're my friends. And the way I look at it, everybody else is pretty busy, too. I'm not the only one who has lots going on."

"You've got drama workshop and student council," Jon said.

"And you've got Computer Club and golf," I said. "At least that's what I heard from Kimber."

"True," said Jon. "I don't know why I thought you were busy every night."

"Maybe it's something somebody said—somebody who may not have the full scoop," I replied.

"Could be," said Jon. And I let it drop at that. He then said, "So . . . what are you doing after school tomorrow?"

"Nothing," I said. Which was before I knew about this meeting with Miss Kattenhorn, of course.

"Then do you want to go with Joannie and me out to see her uncle about the tractor and hay wagon?"

"What do we have to do?" I said. I thought to myself, *Joannie said that would be no problem and that she'd arrange it. What does she need Jon to do?*

"Joannie thought it would be a good idea to see the setup," Jon said.

"Sure," I said boldly. "I'd love to. That will give me a chance to get to know Joannie a little better."

"Good," said Jon. "I'll meet you at the drinking fountain where we met today, OK?"

So, dear Journal, you can probably guess what happened. I raced to the drinking fountain to find Jon and Joannie already there—his last class is only two steps away from it. And I told them what

Miss Kattenhorn had said. Jon quickly responded, "Do you want me to go in with you?"

"That would be great, Jon," I said.

But then Joannie piped up, "Will it take long, Jon? My uncle is going to be waiting for us."

"I probably ought to see what Miss Kattenhorn has to say," Jon said. But Joannie just got this big pout on her face—which really irritated me, I don't mind saying. "I guess we could reschedule with him," Joannie said.

To which good ol' Katelyn said, "Oh, why don't you go on. I can do this by myself."

"Will you call me later to let me know what happened?" Jon said. I could tell he felt pulled in two directions.

"Sure," I said. "No problem."

But, dear Journal, it *is* a problem. And not only with Joannie. That is now very clearly a problem to me. It's plain as day that she has her eyes on Jon. There's absolutely no reason that I can figure out for her to have *needed* Jon to go with her out to her uncle's farm this afternoon. I think she just wanted to have him to herself for a little while, and she certainly didn't seem pleased that I was planning to go along. In fact, I don't think she had a clue that Jon had asked me to go with them.

Back to the more pressing matter, however, of my meeting with Miss Kattenhorn.

It appears that our status as an official club is being seriously questioned. Miss Scaroni apparently told Miss Kattenhorn about our meeting and how smoothly it all went, *and* that she was impressed at how both Jon and Julio had prayed. I must admit, their prayers were really neat. Jon prayed for the school and all the people who might become FF Club members that we would really make a difference in Collinsville. And Julio thanked God for everybody there and asked God to help us be true friends to each other. They were great prayers.

And that's the problem. Miss Kattenhorn said that it's expressly forbidden to include any religious practice or service as a part of any official school club, and she reminded me—a little sternly I might add—that she had told me that very plainly.

"I honestly didn't think of prayer as a religious service," I said to her. "Do you mean that a school club can't even open and close in prayer? As far as I know that's the only mention of God that was made in the whole meeting."

"Precisely," said Miss Kattenhorn. "No prayer."

"But we've always opened and closed our FF Club meetings in prayer," I said.

"Well, then maybe you shouldn't be a school club, Katelyn," she said. I could tell by the tone of her voice that there was absolutely no room for negotiation on this matter as far as she was concerned.

"But don't we have prayer before the football and basketball games?" I asked. Somehow I seemed to recall that.

"Not at Collinsville High," she said. "At least not since the new ruling came out from the superintendent's office last year." I guess it must have been sports events at Castle Rock that I was remembering.

"So if we want to have prayer to start and end our meetings, we can't be a school club," I said, trying to get everything square in my mind—which was reeling. I couldn't fully believe what I was hearing. "But if we don't have prayer, we can be a school club?"

"Yes," Miss Kattenhorn said. "As long as you leave God out of your club, you can be an official school club."

If she had said it any other way, I might have been inclined to go along with what she said, but when she said those words "as long as you leave God out of your club," something inside of me really snapped. God has been a big part of our club. It's largely because of God that we *are* a club, and that we get along so well together as friends.

I was furious inside but I tried to be cool. Oh, how I wish Jon *had* been there with me! I said, "Well, Miss Kattenhorn, I guess we'll have to discuss this again as a club. I'm sorry I misunderstood what you said before. Now that I fully get the picture, we'll probably have to reconsider."

"Well, let me know," she said. "I need to have your answer by the fifteenth."

And of course, dear Journal, there's nobody home when you need them! I tried calling Kimber,

Libby, Trish—even Linda, and then I gave up. By that time, Dad had walked in from work. He could tell immediately that I was pretty upset.

"What's up, Kat-Kat?" he said. It was comforting to hear him use my nickname.

"We aren't going to be able to be an official school club if we open and close our club meetings in prayer," I said.

"You're kidding," he said. "That's the only reason?"

"Yep."

"So how do you feel about that?" Dad asked.

"I'm very *very* mad," I said.

"Angry," Dad said.

"Angry," I repeated. Mom always had a big thing about our saying we were mad. "Mad people live in asylums," she'd say. "Mad people can be angry and angry people can be mad, but mad people and angry people aren't necessarily the same." It was a real Mom-ism.

"What are you going to do?" Dad asked. He has a way of being so logical and to the point.

"Well, we'll just have to drop our application," I said.

"Can you make that decision all by yourself?" Dad asked. He had a point.

"No, I guess not," I admitted. "I guess I'll have to call an emergency meeting of the people who are members of the FF Club—which I guess will have to be held off campus. We'll have to vote on it. But I'm sure everybody will want to withdraw."

"Are you really all that certain?" Dad asked.

"Sure," I said. "Why? Do you think somebody *wouldn't* want to withdraw?"

"I don't know," Dad said. "A month ago I knew all the kids who are in your club, but I don't anymore. You've added several new members in just the last couple of weeks, haven't you?"

"Yes," I said. "Ten."

"Well," said Dad, "that's double the number you had. If majority rules, you might be surprised to find that your club now wants to be an official school club *without* prayer more than an unofficial off-campus club *with* prayer."

That thought had never once entered my mind. We sat down to dinner and our entire conversation was about prayer and whether it should be in school or not. Grandpa Stone was shocked to hear that the school day doesn't begin with prayer anymore. "What's our nation coming to?" he asked, and kept shaking his head.

Kiersten couldn't understand what was so wrong with prayer. "Nothing is wrong with prayer," Aunt Beverly kept saying. And Kiersten just kept asking, "Then why isn't it allowed at school?" There isn't any answer that makes sense, at least as far as I can tell.

Aunt Beverly wondered aloud if perhaps we should talk to the school board about the matter, and Dad brought up the recent rulings of the Supreme Court, and before I knew it, we had sat at the table for over an hour discussing all this.

As soon as the dishes were clear, I called Jon. He didn't even wait to hear what I had to say. He thought I was calling just to check up on the tractor and hay wagon.

"It's really neat," Jon said. "You're going to love this, Katelyn."

"Jon . . . ," I tried to interrupt.

"No, really. Hear me on this. The wagon is loaded with loose hay and there's plenty of room for all of our current members to be on it. We measured for the sign. And Joannie has a great idea that we might all want to wear jeans and country shirts to go along with the overall theme. What do you think?"

"I think we may not be able to do this after all, Jon," I said.

"Why not? I know you aren't big on country stuff, Katelyn, but lots of people are into country big-time. It could be fun just this once to be part of the jeans-and-flannel-shirt crowd," Jon said. I felt like I was listening to a record that I couldn't stop.

"That's not it, Jon," I said.

"Well then, what?" he said. "Joannie said she didn't think you liked the idea and probably wouldn't want to ride the float, but I just laughed her off. Are you that set against it?"

Joannie again!

"No, Jon Weaver," I said, and I knew my voice was louder than it needed to be, but I just couldn't help it. "That isn't it at all. I'm tired of Joannie Field telling everybody what I can and can't do, or what I'm thinking or not thinking. I love the idea of a hay ride, and I love the idea of a hay wagon float. But that's not the problem. If you'd been with me in Miss Kattenhorn's office this afternoon, you'd know that!"

Dead silence on the other end of the line.

I calmed down a little and went on, "Jon, we have a major problem about being an official school club."

"We do?" he asked, and I could hear a little hurt in his voice.

"Yes," I said. "I'm sorry that I yelled at you, but I'm pretty upset about this. I met with Miss Kattenhorn and she said that we can't open and close our meetings in prayer if we're an official school club."

"You're kidding," he said. "We can't be an official school club just because we say a short prayer at the start and end of our meetings?"

"Right," I said. "And if we're not an official school club, we can't have a float in the Homecoming Parade."

"Well, what do you think happens next?" Jon said.

"Me personally," I asked, "or me, club president?"

"Both," said Jon.

"Me personally—I don't think we can be a school club. We've always opened and closed our meetings in prayer and that's part of who we are as the FF Club," I said.

"And you, club president?" Jon asked.

"I think we need to call a special meeting of the club—probably off campus—and talk this over and decide," I said.

"What's to decide?" Jon asked.

"If we want to be a school club," I said.

"But you just said we can't be and have prayer," Jon responded.

"I know, Jon," I said, trying very hard to be patient, and realizing at the same time that Jon was running through the same thoughts that I had been through. "If we have prayer, no club. But if the club votes to drop prayer, we can have an official school club. Miss Kattenhorn put it very clearly, 'If you leave God out of your club, you can be an official school club.' Dad pointed out to me this evening that we have nineteen members now—which means, Jon, that we have more new members than old members. Who knows how the vote will turn out?"

"I'm with you," Jon said. "This could be a major meeting. When do you want to meet?"

"As soon as possible," I said. "We have to decide before the fifteenth and that's not very far away."

"Tomorrow after school?" Jon asked.

"I can't," I said. "First student council meeting. And besides, I think maybe we need to tell people what's happening when we call to tell them about the meeting. That way they can do some thinking about it before they come."

"Thinking . . . and praying," Jon said.

"Right," I said.

"Well, next Monday you have drama workshop, right?" Jon asked. "And we probably can't meet over the weekend. Is next Tuesday too late?"

"What about Friday?" I said.

"Oh, yeah, Friday," Jon said. He seemed a little hesitant. "I guess that would work."

"Did you have something else planned?"

"Well, nothing that can't be postponed a little," he said. I was a little surprised he didn't tell me what he had planned.

We decided that the meeting would be at my house right after school, and that we'd try to keep it as short as possible. As far as we know, only two of the kids who signed up for the club ride the bus, and maybe Dennis can take them home. Jon agreed to phone the new members to tell them about the meeting.

I spent the next hour on the phone, talking to Kimber, Trish, and Libby. They agreed to call Dennis, Ford, Julio, and of course in telling Ford, Linda will know, and she can tell Kent.

I'm wondering if this is something worth bringing up at student council.

Chapter Ten

Important Meetings

Saturday
5 P.M.

*T*he last two days have been packed with school and meetings. I'm glad for an evening to relax without anything I *have* to do. Kimber is coming over a little later. Dennis is going bowling with some of his friends in the Bowling Club and even though Kimber was invited to go along, she hates bowling, so we decided to have a "girls night in."

Student council was interesting. I didn't say anything after all about this matter of praying in clubs. In fact, I didn't say anything at all during the meeting. Most of the meeting was spent discussing some of the activities planned for the year and the duties of being a student council member and class officer. I sat with the other officers from my class and it was good to get to know them a little better. I think I'm going to like Claire a lot. I can see better why she was elected. She has a

101

good sense of humor and yet also a serious side. She spoke up in the meeting when the topic was deciding which events could be officially sponsored by clubs. I thought she made a good point. She'd be a good member for the FF Club . . . I'll have to ask her sometime if she's interested. But I think I'll wait until we make a decision about whether to be an official club. Jason and Chad were very nice to me, but Thomas was off in his own universe. Maybe "class historians" are just like that.

After supper Thursday night, I had a good talk with Dad about the FF Club. I told him that I didn't think this business about prayer was fair at all—after all, we're the ones in the club and we should be able to decide what we want to do, or not do, as a club.

"I don't think anyone's taking that privilege away from you," Dad said.

"But they are," I argued. "They're saying we can't pray and be a club."

"Not really," Dad said. "They're saying that you can't pray and be an *official school* club. You can still be a club. It's the 'official school' part that is in question."

"Do you think that's right?" I asked.

"It's not what I'd like to see," said Dad, "but that's because I'm a Christian and I'd like for all the organizations and institutions that I'm part of to be Christ-centered. And that's just not the case,

Katelyn. We live in a country where people are free to choose *not* to be Christians."

"But don't Christians have any rights?" I asked. "Don't we have a right to choose to have prayer if we want to?"

"Yes," said Dad, "but not in a public institution that is supposed to be accessible to everyone. I wish it was another way . . . but on the other hand, how would you feel if you went to—say, an English Club meeting at school, and the meeting opened and closed with the entire group falling on its knees toward Mecca and reciting prayers in Arabic?"

"I wouldn't join that club," said Katelyn.

"Even if it was an English Club that did lots of activities that you wanted to do?" Dad asked.

"No," I said, "I wouldn't join."

"But do you think it's right for an English Club at school to allow a few people in the club to dictate that Islamic prayers would be part of the club? What if you joined and then the club officers made that rule?"

"I see what you mean," I said. "No, I don't think that's right. But what if the people know up-front, before they join, that the club has prayers?"

"I think the school's position would be that a student should have an equal option to belong to a club that didn't have any religious overtones. For example, if there's an FF Club that prays, then there should be an FF Club that doesn't pray, so that students could decide between them."

"That would be a waste . . . to have two FF Clubs."

"That's precisely the school's point. There should be just one club, and rather than make anyone feel uncomfortable about God and religion, they are saying that God and religion should be left out of school clubs."

"But what if the entire club voted unanimously to have prayers after they were all members?" I asked.

"I don't know," said Dad. "I'm not sure that's ever been put to the test. That's not the case with the FF Club, though, is it?"

"No," I said. "At least not yet." I felt as if I was trying to hatch an idea that just wouldn't hatch.

"I think part of the problem, Katelyn, is that you and your friends formed this club early in the summer, and at that point, you could decide for yourselves just what you wanted the club to be and to do. Each time you add a new member, you have one more person who is going to help with the deciding."

"I've been afraid all along of getting too big," I said.

"I don't think size is the issue," Dad said. "At least not the major issue. I think it's more a matter of control. The bigger the club, and the more new members you add, the less control you who started the club are going to have. I'm not sure you've ever faced that prospect."

"You're right," I said, "we haven't. I think we all saw adding members as a way of having more friends. In a way, I think we just assumed that all of the new members would fit in with us perfectly, and that we'd all get along just like we have up till now."

"That may or may not be the case," Dad said. "You're going to have to face the possibility that a big club is going to mean that you can't know everybody equally well. And that if you're going to be an official school club, you're going to have to play by school rules."

"Don't you think it's possible to change the school rules, Dad?" I asked.

"Perhaps," Dad said. "But changing rules takes time and commitment. I don't think you're going to be able to change the rules before the end of September."

"Probably not."

"In fact, you might not be able to change the rules for several years. It would take a long effort, I think."

"What do you think would happen if we just went ahead and prayed anyway—or maybe had a 'silent' prayer?" I asked.

"I think that would be rebellion, Katelyn," Dad said. "As Christians, we're to live under authority and play by the rules that have been established, until such time as we can influence authority and get the laws changed. The only time we have an example of someone in the Bible doing otherwise is when there was absolutely no allowance at all in the law for worship of God—as when the king decreed that nobody could pray *at all* and Daniel went ahead and prayed. Even then, he had to suffer the consequences . . ."

"Yeah . . . being thrown in a lions' den," I said. "Yuck."

"I agree, but his stand was important and it was very personal. Daniel's protest didn't involve anybody but Daniel, if you remember. He acted on his own personal convictions," Dad said. "And even though God protected Daniel, Daniel was still subject to the king's authority and the punishment of the law."

"Isn't there anything we can do to let the school know that we think this is a bad rule?"

"Well, you can always protest this ruling, but I don't think you are right willfully to break it. Do you see the difference?" Dad asked.

"Yes," I said. "Unfortunately." We were both quiet for a minute, watching the fire crackle away in the fireplace. It was a pretty cold night. Fall is really here. Kiersten came in wearing bright pink flannel pajamas and went over to sit on Dad's lap, all the while combing the hair on her doll.

"Well," I asked, "what do you think about the idea of our voting *not* to have prayer and becoming an official school club and then working hard to get the rules changed?"

"You might try that," Dad said, "but in my experience, once a group has compromised on a point like that, pretty soon the group learns to 'live with' whatever they compromised."

"You don't think we'd stick with our goal of getting the rule changed?" I asked. "We can be pretty stubborn."

"True, but it's hard to sustain that kind of commitment," Dad said. "It's not impossible, but I think you all would have to make this your top priority. It would probably have to be *the* purpose for your club. And as such, it would probably keep you from getting a lot of other things done—both as a club, and you personally. You've got a lot of irons in the fire right now, Katelyn."

"So what do you think we should do?" I asked.

"I think that's up to you and your friends," Dad said. "I do think you should consider both options that are open to you right now."

"To drop prayer and be a school club," I said, "or to keep prayer and not be a school club."

"Don't overlook the fact that you could keep prayer and be an off-campus community club," Dad said.

"Same difference," I said.

"Yes," said Dad, "and no. You keep saying, 'and not be a school club.' I think your two options might be better stated as, 'drop prayer and be an official school club,' or 'keep prayer and be the community club we started out to be.'"

"You're right!" I said. And suddenly, dear Journal, it all became very clear. The FF Club didn't start out to be a school club. It started as a *friends* club—a club we started to do good projects for Collinsville and have fun together as friends at the same time. We don't *need* to be a school club to continue doing what we did all summer!

"Do you think we could still have a hay ride?" I asked, already knowing the answer.

"Why not?" Dad said.

"Of course!" I said. "And we could make it the hay ride we want—not just part of a Homecoming Parade but a real hay ride—with marshmallows and a campfire and singing."

"Sounds fun to me," Dad said. "Need a chaperone?"

"And then Kiersten and Mari could go, too," I said. Kiersten looked up from her combing and beamed a huge smile at me. "I *like* this idea," she said.

"*If* your club planned it that way," Dad said. Kiersten looked up at him with a scowl, which caused Dad to give her nose a tweak.

Oh, dear Journal, it all makes so much more sense this way. We don't have to fight the system— we can operate as a *different* system. Maybe I can work on the student council to get the rules changed, and we could still have the FF Club and activities outside school. I tried to call Jon right then and there, but his line was busy. I guess he was trying to call the new members to tell them about Friday's meeting. I thought about it too late, but I should have been the one to volunteer to call Joannie. As it was, Jon had that responsibility. I hope that's not who he was talking to for so long on Thursday night.

Anyway . . . dear Journal. That was part one of my two days of important meetings. Friday was the actual FF Club meeting.

We met at our house right after school—sixteen of us showed up. One of our club members, Joey, had to go home to get ready to go to a family wedding. Jon had talked to him and Joey said that he'd like to be a part of the FF Club either way—whether we were official or not. He told Jon that he's not particularly religious, but he said it didn't bother him that we had prayer. In fact, he thought it was kind of neat that we did. The other person who wasn't there was a girl named Jill. We don't know why she wasn't at the meeting. Kent also couldn't be there, but Linda said that he agreed to vote whatever way she did. So, in a way, we had seventeen of our nineteen members represented.

The discussion we had was really hot at times. It was just as Dad had suspected, or at least how I *think* he suspected. Six of the new members spoke up loud and clear and said they thought we should be a school club, and it didn't matter to them at all that we would not be having prayer at the beginning and ending of our meetings.

All of us who were old members—the "originals" as Libby calls us—said we thought prayer was important, and that we'd rather be an "unofficial" club and have prayer, than to be an official one without prayer. At first, Dennis thought it might be OK to quit the opening and closing prayers. His argument was that he thought we might be able to do more good as an official school club than an unofficial one, and that it might be worth sacrificing prayer in order to get those things done.

Kimber said she thought that the issue was not just prayer, but "leaving God out." She said she was very uncomfortable with that, and pointed out that over the summer, we had talked about God quite a bit when we got together and that it would be hard to forget when we were being "official" and when we were just hanging out together as Christian friends. I was very glad to see Kimber speak up that way. I was a little afraid that she'd just go along with whatever Dennis said.

Joannie was one of the first ones to speak up in favor of dropping prayer and remaining a school club. I watched Jon while she spoke and I could see that he was quite upset at what she was saying. He also seemed a little stunned, as if he couldn't quite believe his ears. Frankly, I wasn't all that surprised.

Unfortunately, several of the other new members sided with Joannie immediately. Julio pointed out that the club was originally started with prayer and lots of freedom to talk about God, which didn't do anything but alienate the new members. They said they thought this was a club in which

110

all members could have an equal voice, and Julio had to admit that it was.

Joannie then argued that none of the other clubs had prayer and they still did a lot of good things and had a lot of fun together. She finally said, "I don't see what the big fuss is all about. So we don't pray. What difference does that make?"

Jon started to say something but hardly got half a word out of his mouth before Trish stood up, and she was more than a little upset.

"It makes a very big difference, Joannie," Trish said. And then Trish went on to give a very strong statement about how she hadn't been all that comfortable in the beginning with all our talk about God and prayer. "The main reason," she said, "was that I really didn't want God in my life right then. So I certainly didn't feel comfortable with God being talked about so much in the club. But the prayers of my friends made a big difference in my life, Joannie. If they hadn't been so open in praying and in telling me what they believe about God and His love, I'm not sure I would have asked God back into my life. One of the best times we've ever had together—at least from my point of view— was when we prayed together on my Gram's front porch. I just can't imagine this club *without* prayer."

"But was that a club event?" Joannie asked. She almost sounded like an attorney.

"I think it was," said Trish. "We had been painting some of the playground equipment at the park and then the club offered to paint Gram's picket fence. We were having refreshments afterward, so I think you could say we were still being a 'club' at that point."

Joannie didn't say anything, and Trish concluded, "I think it's pretty serious when we say that God can't be part of something. Maybe in some things that's OK. But in this club, I don't think it's right." I wanted to give a cheer for Trish, but I somehow managed to stay quiet.

Jon finally stood up and asked the newcomers if any of them objected to prayer or were offended by it. Nobody said anything, but I noticed that Joannie kept her eyes on the floor at that point. He then asked, "How many of you would want to be part of the FF Club if it *wasn't* an official school club?"

One of the new members, a guy named Mark, asked what we would do differently if we weren't an official school club. Jon looked at me and I said, "Probably nothing would change from the way we have been doing things. We couldn't have a float in the Homecoming Parade and we couldn't sponsor an official school event or party. On the other hand, we could do just as much for Collinsville, and we could have parties and events and sponsor projects just like we did last summer. And we could feel free to talk about anything we want, including religion and God."

A girl named Margee said she didn't think she could be a part because she has to ride the bus and it sounded as if we'd be doing things on weekends and in town where she might not be able to participate.

Joannie said she thought that was a very important point—that not everybody could come to everything if we weren't an official school club. Jon surprised me at that point by asking Joannie point-blank, "Would you still want to be part of the FF Club, Joannie, if we weren't an official school club?"

"Would you want me to be a member, Jon?" she asked.

"I hope you'd want to be a member, Joannie," said Jon. She really beamed when he said that, but she wasn't prepared, I don't think, for what Jon said next. "But I wouldn't hold it against you if you decided you couldn't be a member." A little pout replaced her grin.

Finally I said, "Listen, I think we have only two choices here. Either we choose to be an official school club and drop prayer from our meetings and make a very serious attempt to keep God out of the FF Club—and I need to emphasize that point. Miss Kattenhorn doesn't want *any* mention of God in our club if we're an official school club. Or . . . we stay the way we've been from the beginning—a club of friends that wants to do service projects for Collinsville. If we stay the way we've been, we don't have to change anything about prayer or talking about God."

Libby said, "I think you're r-r-right, Katelyn.

This isn't really about being 'official' or 'unofficial.' This is about being the k-k-kind of club we want to be." Several people nodded or seemed to be in agreement so I said in my very official president's voice, "Do I hear a motion?"

Jon said, "I move that we remain the club we have been and withdraw our application to be an official school club." Trish seconded his motion even before I could say anything.

We took a vote and the ayes and nays sounded about even. I didn't quite know what to do, but Julio piped up and said, "I think we need a show of hands." So that's what we did. The vote was eight to eight. Linda raised two hands and Joannie said she didn't think that was fair since we didn't know for *sure* that Kent had said Linda could vote for him. Jon looked at her and said, "I believe Linda and besides that, I talked to Kent during lunch today and he said that he wanted Linda to have his proxy vote." (I learned a new word—proxy!) Joannie just glared at Jon and didn't say anything. I could tell she definitely wasn't amused.

The point was, it was a tie vote, eight to eight. We've never had any vote that wasn't unanimous in the FF Club. Once again, I didn't know what to do, but Julio came to my rescue a second time, "It's a tie. So you need to cast the deciding ballot, Katelyn." I realized I had been so busy counting votes that I hadn't cast my own vote.

I've got to admit, dear Journal, when it came right down to my making the decision, it wasn't easy. I looked at all the new kids who wanted to be in the club and they had all voted *against* the motion. They wanted us to be an official school club. As I looked at them, I thought, *I'd like to be friends with these kids and I certainly don't want them to be mad at me. Several of them really helped me get elected as sophomore class secretary.* Still, all but Dennis of the old kids had voted for the motion—which meant we'd stay the way we have been from the beginning. And these are my friends.

"What's your vote?" Jon asked again. "Is God in or out of the club?" I was so glad he put it just that way. It made my vote very easy.

I said, "God's in our club, Jon. I vote for your motion." A half-cheer went up from the ones who had voted for the motion, but I started to speak so they wouldn't get too enthusiastic. I looked straight at the new kids and said, "I almost voted against the motion because I really want you to be my friends and to be in this club. I want you to know that I'm going to work very hard on the student council to get this rule changed. But until it is changed, I don't think I can compromise on this and vote to keep God out of the FF Club. I hope you'll still want to be a part and that we won't have any hard feelings."

Joannie said, "Well, I'll still be a part." Two or three others said, "Me, too." I told the new kids that if any one of them wanted out of the club, just to let Jon, or Libby, or me know and we'd take their name off the club roster. Otherwise, we'd assume that everybody wanted to stay a part. Even Margee said she'd think about it over the weekend.

And that's the way it went. Dennis made a motion that we adjourn the meeting. Everybody got up to get ready to leave. Trish came up and gave me a big hug and Julio boomed out in his happy-go-lucky way, "Hugs all around!" So we introduced the new kids to another FF Club custom—hugs to everybody.

After the meeting, I noticed that Joannie left the house with Jon. I don't know if she was going somewhere with him, or they just walked out together, but when I tried to call Jon later in the evening, he wasn't home.

It was not until today at The Wonderful Life Shop that I found out that he *had* gone somewhere with Joannie—he and Joannie and Aunt Beverly and Mr. Clark Weaver had gone to Mexico Pete's for dinner!

I don't mind telling you, dear Journal, that I was very *very* upset when I heard that. Jon taking Joannie to the place we've always gone for dinner as friends? And with Aunt Beverly?

On the other hand, I was very happy to hear that Aunt Beverly and Mr. Clark Weaver had gone somewhere together. Aunt Beverly said she was glad, too. She seemed a little happier this week than last week. I think the store is all coming together in pretty good order. We stopped by there before we came to the shop this morning and things are looking *very* nice.

Aunt Beverly was pretty casual about the dinner at Mexico Pete's, though. She said Mr. Clark Weaver had called her and asked her if she could take a "fun break" and have tacos with him and Jon. So she met them at Mexico Pete's and Mr. Clark Weaver showed up with Joannie and Jon. She didn't seem to think that it was any big deal that Joannie and Jon were together. In fact, she said that she liked Joannie—I think her words were, "She's very clever, Katelyn."

"Clever doesn't necessarily mean good," I said.

"I didn't say good, Katie," said Aunt Beverly. "I said 'clever.' She's a girl who's used to having things her way and getting what she wants, and I suspect she has a big bag of tricks she's used for years to develop that talent."

"Do you think Jon likes her?" I asked.

"I don't know," said Aunt Beverly. "He wasn't all that buddy-buddy with her, not nearly as free in communicating as he is with you. He seemed a little uncomfortable, actually—maybe it was because I was there, too. He didn't say very much, and I certainly didn't see much of the old Jon Weaver grin."

That told me a lot. If Jon wasn't grinning, he wasn't having all that good a time. It's hard for me to imagine Jon *not* teasing and grinning.

I came straight home after work—Aunt Beverly suggested that I leave at four o'clock today. I had worked through the lunch hour to cover for her while she went to see if the sign at the new store had been installed correctly. I took a long hot bubble bath, and now, it's time for dinner . . . and for Kimber to show up. I'm glad she's coming over.

Chapter Eleven

Girl Talk

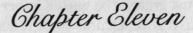

Sunday
4 P.M.

*K*imber came over about seven-thirty on Saturday night and ended up staying the night. We curled up in front of the fireplace and talked until almost one o'clock in the morning. That's the latest I've stayed up in months! We both had a tough time getting up and going to church today. That's why I just awoke from a nice long Sunday-afternoon nap!

Dad let Kimber and me make hot chocolate and two big batches of popcorn. Kimber and I also brought down the big pillows from the guest bed and we made our own little "nest" there in the living room in front of the fire. He and Kiersten went out to see a movie—yet another version of *The Three Musketeers*. Kiersten just loves that story. I think there must be four or five versions of that movie and we've seen them all!

It was just great to be with Kimber again. She's been so busy with Dennis for the last couple of months that we haven't had a lot of girl-talk time, except on the phone. It's true that I talk to her every day, either at school or on the phone, but I've been missing our talks that go on hour after hour. Aunt Beverly calls it "serious girl talk"—the kind of talk when you can really share your heart.

Kimber's still crazy about Dennis, of course. But they've been dating now for long enough that she's able to see some of his quirks and faults. "He drives me nuts sometimes," she said at one point in our talk. "I have to remember that I probably drive him nuts, too."

Kimber's parents still don't want her to go out with Dennis on a date without another couple or a group of kids going along. But that doesn't seem to cramp Kimber's style. "Actually, it makes it easier," she said. "Dennis kisses me good night every time we go out, but I don't have to worry about things getting too intense."

"Do you ever wish you could go out with someone else?" I asked.

"I wonder sometimes what it would be like to have a different boyfriend," Kimber admitted, "but frankly, I can't think of anybody I'd rather be with than Dennis. Dennis isn't all that romantic, but he's a really nice guy and he's nice to me and we have a lot of fun together."

"What do you mean, not romantic?" I said. I was a little surprised to hear her say that.

"Well, you know, he's not like Julio is to Libby," she said.

"Julio is romantic? To Libby?" I said. "Where *have* I been, Kimber? Do I live on some other planet? Why isn't anybody telling me anything?"

"I'm sure Libby will tell you everything," Kimber laughed, "as soon as you can get her to spend an evening off the phone with Julio!"

"So what does he do that's so romantic?" I said.

"Oh, he'll bring her a flower at school, or make a tape of a song for her, or write her a little note telling her that he thinks she did something wonderful," Kimber said.

"He does? That's really neat. I just wouldn't have thought it of Julio."

"He's very sweet. I think he's only kissed Libby a couple of times," she said, "but that's all right with Libby right now. She said she wants to take things slow."

"He's kissed her?" I asked. "Now I really do feel left out."

"Just a couple of times, Katelyn," Kimber said. "Once was on the cheek, so I'm not sure that counts. She seemed excited about it, but actually, she didn't say all that much. Whenever I bring up Julio, she just gets this faraway look in her eyes. I think she likes him a whole lot, but she's almost afraid to talk about it for fear that it will somehow all evaporate into thin air."

"I know how she feels," I said.

There must have been something different in

my voice, because Kimber picked up on it right away. "So what is it that you aren't talking about for fear it will evaporate?" she asked.

"I think it's more my being afraid to say something for fear that it might be true," I said. "You know, if you don't say anything, it's easier to convince yourself that you might be imagining something that will go away."

"Like what?" Kimber pressed. I didn't say anything for a minute.

"Do you want more hot chocolate?" I finally asked.

"In a minute. I'll get it," Kimber said. "Like *what*, Katelyn?"

"Like Jon and Joannie," I admitted.

"What are you afraid about?"

"That they're becoming a couple," I said with a sigh.

"And that bothers you?" Kimber asked.

"I don't like to admit it, I guess, but it does bother me. I don't think Joannie is right for Jon. There's something about her that bugs me," I said.

"I'm so glad to hear you say that," Kimber said.

"Why?" I asked. "Does something bug you about Joannie?"

"No, not really," she said. "I think Joannie has some great qualities, and also some problems, but that's not what I meant. I'm glad you're *upset* about all the time Joannie manages to spend with Jon. I was beginning to think you were either blind or that you didn't care at all!"

"What do you mean 'manages to spend'?" I asked.

"Well, it's Joannie who seems to be engineering all the time they spend together," said Kimber. "It's plain as day. She's got a huge crush on Jon and she's forever suggesting that they go places together or do things together. She always makes it sound just important enough for Jon to agree to go, but I'm not sure he really wants to go."

"Well, he wanted to go enough to take her to Mexico Pete's for dinner last night," I said.

"I'm glad you know about that," Kimber said. "I wasn't sure whether to tell you. But that's just a good example of what I mean."

"How so?"

"Well, when we were over at Jon's house a few days ago, Mr. Weaver came home and I heard Joannie say to him in the kitchen, 'I hope I have a chance to get to know you a little better, Mr. Weaver. Jon says so many wonderful things about you.'" Kimber was doing a fabulous imitation of Joannie's voice at that point. I had to giggle.

"And what happened?"

"Mr. Weaver said, 'Good idea, Joannie. I'd like to get to know you a little better, too. Why don't you and Jon join me for dinner Friday night? I'll treat you all to enchiladas at Mexico Pete's.'"

"So Jon wasn't the one who asked Joannie to go?" I said. I felt a tremendous sense of relief, I don't mind saying.

"No, not at all. It was all Joannie's idea. What could Jon have said?"

I thought to myself, *He could have said no,* but I quickly realized that he really couldn't have said that without causing a scene. And there was nothing to cause a scene over. Jon was stuck. I felt a little sorry for him, actually.

"Do you think Jon likes Joannie?" I asked. I was almost too scared to hear her answer.

"Only as a friend," Kimber said. "Nothing more . . . at least from what I can tell."

Only as a friend. That's the way he likes me, too. "Jon really is a good friend to have," I said.

At which point Kimber said something that made me feel very *very* happy. "He doesn't like her the way he likes you, Katelyn," Kimber said. "Everybody but you, it seems, can see that Jon's crazy about you. And frankly, I think you're crazy about him, too. I wish you guys would just admit that to each other. It would make life a lot easier for all of us."

"Do you really think so?" I said, getting up to put another log on the fire.

"Sure," Kimber said. "That way Dennis and I could double-date with you and Jon. I think it would be a blast for us to double-date."

"That's not what I meant," I said, although I thought the idea of double-dating with Dennis and Kimber sounded like a great idea, too. "I meant, do you really think Jon likes me as more than just a friend?"

"Yes, I do," Kimber said very seriously. "And I think you know it and are just scared to admit it because you feel the same way about him. Joannie wouldn't make you jealous at all if you didn't like him as more than a friend."

"Maybe you're right," I said. "I've been having a terrible time even wanting to try to get to know Joannie better, much less be a true friend to her. Maybe I have been a little jealous."

"So go for it," Kimber said.

"You mean go for Jon?" I asked.

"Who else?" she said with a grin, helping herself to another bowl of popcorn.

"I'm not sure how to go about that, Kimber," I said. "Jon and I have been good friends and only good friends up to this point. I'm not sure how to go about telling him that I really like him more than all my other guy friends. He'd probably think I was just saying that I wanted to be *best* friends with him, not that I like him as a boyfriend."

"You'll find a way," said Kimber. "You guys have always been able to talk."

Kimber's right, dear Journal. Jon and I *have* been able to talk. About everything, it seems. Except liking each other as boyfriend and girlfriend.

When we finally went to bed at one o'clock, Kimber went right to sleep, but I stayed awake for almost another hour, thinking about Jon and all the good times we've had together. He really is quite a guy, that Jon Weaver. I realized that just thinking about him made me smile.

Chapter Twelve

A New Plan

Sunday
9 P.M.

I just got back from youth group at church. All the old-timer FF Club kids were there, plus Kent (who naturally came with Linda). We had a blast together. Everybody seems very *relieved* that we aren't going to be an official school club.

Pastor Bert and Pastor Sharyn could see that we were all pretty excited about something so they asked us what we were all feeling so "up" about, and we told them about the school ruling and our decision to keep the FF Club an off-campus community club. Rather than follow through on what they had planned, Bert and Sharyn spent the entire youth group time—after singing a few choruses—talking about what had happened, and about the importance of standing up for a Christian witness at school. Bert and Sharyn seemed really pleased at the choice we all had made.

"We've got some f-f-fences to mend, though," said Libby.

"Right," said Julio. "About half the club members voted to be an official school club and those kids are really neat kids. We need to try to keep them in the club."

So we talked about that a little, too.

Finally Pastor Sharyn asked, "Are you still going to have your hay ride?"

"I hope so," I said. "I think maybe we have a chance to make this something even better than we thought originally."

"It could be our next FF Club project," Jon said.

"Great!" said Trish. "I was really looking forward to that hay wagon ride. That's the one part I was sorry to see go—our chance to be in the Homecoming Parade and dress up country style."

"You wear jeans all the time anyway," Ford said with a grin. "At least, jeans skirts."

"But I'm not exactly into the country look," Trish said and we all grinned. Trish's look is much more uptown casual—with her bright T-shirts and glitzy baseball caps.

"So what kind of hay ride did you have in mind?" Julio asked. "I'm all for a party!" When isn't Julio ready for a party! He's always eager to celebrate something.

"Do you have some ideas?" Jon asked.

I told the group about the kind of hay rides that Aunt Beverly and Dad had described for me—with a campfire and roasting marshmallows. "We could still sing and ride the hay wagon to and from the campfire site," I concluded.

"Sounds like fun," Kimber said.

"When's the next full moon?" Dennis asked as Kimber jabbed him in the ribs with her elbow.

"I don't know," I said, "but I can check. Grandpa Stone is always up on that."

"We just had a full moon about two weeks ago," Bert said. "So it's probably about two weeks from now."

"That's plenty of time to plan something," Trish said.

"But what's our good cause?" Ford said. "We've been talking about our club tonight and part of the reason for our club is to do something for Collinsville. I'm all in favor of a hay ride, but how does it fit into our reason for being a club?"

"We could charge admission to the hay ride," Linda suggested, "and then give the money to something worthwhile."

And that's when it hit me, dear Journal. "I think I might know just the thing!" I said. (I think my voice might have been just a little too loud on that line, but nobody seemed to notice.)

I told the group about Emily, and about what had happened to her on a hay ride. Everybody got real quiet and Kimber said, "I think that's one of the saddest stories I've ever heard."

I told them about the little garden across the park at school and then I said, "Maybe we could call this the Emily Pearson Memorial Hay Ride, and use the money to do something that would help keep kids from drinking."

"You mean like give the money to MADD?" Jon asked.

"Who's mad?" Julio asked.

"It's M-A-D-D," I said, "Mothers Against Drunk Driving. Our family has been a member of that organization ever since Mom was killed in a car accident by a drunk driver who ran a stoplight. We could make a donation to MADD, but we also might want to do something else that would be a little more geared only to Collinsville."

"So what's the night when everybody drinks too much?" Ford asked. Everybody had a different idea, so Ford finally answered his own question, "New Year's Eve! Maybe we could use the money to have a no-alcohol New Year's Eve party somewhere in Collinsville—and invite the whole town."

"Two parties!" Julio said with a big grin. We all laughed, but I could see that things were really cooking.

"The main thing," Jon said, "is to get the hay ride going so we take advantage of the next full moon. November will be too cold, probably. It's got to be in October. We can decide later what to do with the money."

"Right," said Libby. "Let's make p-p-plans."

So we did. In a way, it's as if the entire youth group—which was really only about ten kids more than our old members—became the FF Club for a few minutes. A couple of the kids who aren't in the FF Club asked me after youth group what it takes to join the club, and the others all said they want to go on the hay ride. So . . . we divided up some responsibilities and we invited Bert and Sharyn to come along as our guests and to lead a devotional time at the campfire.

This is going to be fun! And best of all, it's going to be *our* kind of hay ride.

Oh, yes, one more thing. Jon said that he thought I should share Emily's story at the campfire. I said that I was planning to write a little play about what happened to Emily. Jon said he thought that was a great idea and maybe we could act it out. After youth group, Jon came over to me and asked, "When's rehearsal?"

"What do you mean?" I said.

"Well, when does The Weave show up at your house to learn his lines?" he said with a grin.

"Wednesday night," I said without even stopping to think about it. "Seven o'clock."

"I'll be there," he said. "Need me to recruit any other dramatic experts?"

"Nope," I said. "I'll do my own casting for this one."

Dear Journal, I am so excited about this. I've already written one page of the play and now I'm eager to really get going on it. I hope I can get a draft done by Wednesday! I'd better!

Chapter Thirteen

Rehearsal

*I*t's another busy week, but I think I'm starting to hit my stride. Things seem to be getting done and I have a much better grip on things than I had two weeks ago. I still have a lot to do, but somehow it all seems to be getting done and I feel less frazzled about it. That's a great feeling! The weather has been absolutely wonderful—bright sunshine and cold mornings. Frost, even! And the leaves are glorious.

School is going all right. I got an *A* on my first paper in Honors English. Algebra is another story, but mostly I'm getting *B*'s in that class. It's a good thing I'm keeping up with all my homework. In theater shop, the sets are starting to take shape. We had a really fun time painting one of the backdrops on Monday afternoon.

Mrs. Davidson, my drama teacher, asked me if

I was going to try out for a part in *The Unsinkable Molly Brown* and I told her that I just didn't think I had time right now. She asked me seriously to reconsider trying out and see if I couldn't find a way to work it into my schedule. I was feeling a little pressure about that, but when I brought up what she said at the dinner table on Monday night, both Dad and Aunt Beverly registered major complaints. Dad simply said, "If you do that, Katelyn, what are you going to drop?" When I told them I hadn't planned on dropping anything I'm doing, Aunt Beverly got very serious and asked me to list all of the things I'm currently doing and how much time each thing takes. She agreed with Dad that I'm booked solid for this semester and in the end, I could see they are right. If I was to get a part in the play, I'd have more than a full plate.

"But what if my teacher holds this against me?" I asked them. I was pretty concerned about that. After all, she gives out the grades.

"Is being in the play a requirement for your class?" Dad asked.

"No," I said. "Only to work in the set shop."

"Then I don't think she'll hold it against you," Aunt Beverly said. "A play is just like going out for a sports team. You might have a physical education teacher who is also a coach, but because you don't go out for a team doesn't mean that you get a lousy grade in physical education."

She was right, as usual. It helps to have someone to talk to about things like this. And Aunt

Beverly always seems to be there . . . along with Dad, of course.

So I told Mrs. Davidson in class on Tuesday that I just couldn't work a play into my schedule this fall. And she said, "Maybe next spring. You'd be a real asset, Katelyn," and left it at that. She wasn't upset at all. And what she said made me feel good.

I also told Miss Scaroni on Monday—between school and set shop—about what the club had decided. Jon had told her we were having our meeting, and he had also told her our decision, but I thought it was only proper for me to tell her also since I'm club president. She was glad I came by and said that she understood completely. And then she said, "I admire the stand you all have taken in the FF Club. I agree with you that this concern over prayer in school has grown way out of proportion, and I hope you *will* be able to bring this up in student council. If there's anything I can do to help you with the FF Club, just let me know. I believe in what you are doing for our town." Now, that made me feel *really* good . . . and Jon seemed especially happy about it, too, when I told him later what Miss Scaroni had said.

Miss Kattenhorn was not quite as supportive, but she wasn't angry or upset either. She said, "I think that's a wise decision, all things considered, and I'm glad you came to tell me, Katelyn. I hope the FF Club has a very successful year. You have a lot of talented students in your club."

So—I felt like I was home free! I worked hard on my play on Monday night and Tuesday night, and by the time Wednesday rolled around, I was ready with a draft for us to read in parts.

I decided to make one character a reporter who interviews Grandpa Stone about the night that Emily was killed. Ford has agreed to play the part of the reporter. And Jon, after a lot of coaxing on my part, has agreed to play Grandpa Stone.

Jon was very reluctant at first. I think he was willing to do the part, he just didn't think he *could* do it. "But I know your Grandpa," he kept saying. "What if he doesn't like the way I play him?"

"He'd like whatever *you* do, Jon," I said. "And besides, there's really no major acting to do. You just have to sit at the table with the reporter and talk. You're good at that!" (I couldn't help teasing him with that last line.)

"I'll give it a try, but if this flops, I warned you," he said.

While Ford is interviewing Jon in the play, two or three kids are going to mime some action in another part of the stage area. Trish has agreed to be Emily Pearson. And Julio is going to play the part of the guy who tries to get Emily drunk. Dennis is going to be the farmhand who originally drives the team of horses, and I asked Kent if he'd be the guy who drives the rig down the wrong road. Everybody was very happy to be asked and Trish told me at lunch today that she practiced

134

falling and dying for two hours last night! "I don't want to hurt myself," she said with a laugh.

Libby and Linda are going to help me with lights and sound effects, and Kimber is going to try to find some old-fashioned clothes to use as costumes.

You'll probably notice, dear Journal, that there are only two speaking parts in this play: the reporter that Ford plays—I'm calling him Mr. Robertson—and Grandpa Stone. That meant, of course, that only Jon and Ford needed to come over last night for rehearsal. In asking the other kids to have a part, I also asked them if they could come over on Saturday night for a full-blown dress rehearsal. That will give me two more days to get the play polished. They all said they could come. (Mrs. Miller told me this afternoon that she's already got a special cake planned for Saturday night! Yum! Her cakes are something else. I keep telling her I think she should open a bakery, but then again, what would we do for a housekeeper?)

As it turned out, Jon showed up alone! He said Ford called him and said he was having major problems with his printer and that he had a big paper due the next day and needed to get his printer fixed and the paper printed out, or he felt he'd be in big trouble in his economics class.

So I read the reporter's part and Jon read Grandpa Stone's part. Jon liked the play right away, which made me feel good. And in reading the play out loud, I realized that several lines needed to be reworded. What looks good on paper sometimes doesn't sound that natural when it's spoken. I can see where reading a play out loud is an important part of *writing* a play.

Jon did a great job of being Grandpa Stone. I told him how Grandpa had paused occasionally in telling us the story, and how he got a faraway look in his eyes. Jon tried that and he did it *perfectly!* We agreed that he doesn't have to memorize his lines. He's going to have them on a sheet of paper at the table where he's sitting during the "interview." And Ford won't have to memorize his lines either. He can have them written down on the notepad he's holding and supposedly using for taking notes.

After three readings through, Jon had everything down pat, so we took a break to have some hot chocolate.

"This is a really good play," Jon said. "I'm pretty impressed at how you've written it."

"Sure," I said. I couldn't quite tell if Jon was teasing or not, so I assumed that he was!

"I'm serious," he said, and sure enough, he wasn't grinning. "You're a good writer, Katelyn. And this play is going to make a lot of kids stop and think."

"Do you really think so?" I said.

"Yes," said Jon "I do. Otherwise I wouldn't have said so." And then he added something very special, "I've always been honest with you, Katelyn."

136

"I know," I said. "It's one of the things I like best about you, Jon Weaver."

"And I appreciate the fact that you are always upfront and honest with me," Jon said.

"I try to be," I said.

"Can I be honest with you about Joannie for a minute?" he said. I must admit, dear Journal, my heart about stopped at that point. I wasn't prepared at all for him to ask that question. I felt this huge lump in my throat. *What was Jon going to say?*

"Sure," I said, trying very *very* hard to sound casual.

"Your aunt may have told you already, but I had dinner with your aunt and Dad and Joannie at Mexico Pete's last Friday night."

"Aunt Beverly told me," I said.

"I thought she might," he said. "I want you to know that going there for dinner with her wasn't my idea. Dad and Joannie kind of rigged it up without talking to me about it."

"It's OK if you go to Mexico Pete's with Joannie," I said.

"I guess so," Jon said. "But it felt strange to be there with Dad and your aunt, and not have you there." I didn't tell him that it felt plenty strange to me, too.

"Do you like Joannie?" I asked Jon, almost afraid for an answer, but then again, we were being "honest" with each other.

"Just as a friend," Jon said.

"Like us," I said, trying to be very matter-of-fact.

"Well, not exactly," Jon said. "I don't know Joannie like I know you, Katelyn."

That was mildly comforting. But then Jon added, "And I probably never will. You're more than 'just a friend,' even though I guess that's our official line. Joannie is a friend, as in, a little above a good acquaintance."

Defining relationships can be so hard at times, dear Journal! And what did Jon mean by saying, "I guess that's our official line"? Does he wish that it wasn't the case? That's not the statement I picked up on, though.

"What do you mean by 'probably never will'?" I asked, getting up to pour him a second cup of hot chocolate. I was glad he couldn't see my face since I knew I probably looked scared. I can't tell you how much I wanted Jon to tell me that he *doesn't* want to be a couple with Joannie.

"Well," said Jon, "I'm not sure how to say this. I don't want to put Joannie down, but sometimes I don't think she tells me the whole story. It's as if she leaves out little things—which sometimes are actually pretty big things—and I can never tell if she's doing that on purpose or by accident. She's too smart to be an air-head that would forget some details, and she's had too many successes to be a person who doesn't follow through on the things she says she's going to do."

"Do you feel as if she's manipulating things

sometimes in order to have things go her way?" I asked, my back still turned to Jon.

"A little. Sometimes," Jon said. I knew it was a real stretch for him to say something that was even that negative about another person. "Nothing ever seems to be real straightforward. There's always this little bit of mystery around the edges that leaves me guessing."

"That could be intriguing," I said, returning to the table to sit down with Jon. I came real close to spilling hot chocolate in his lap. "A lot of guys seem to like that. They think it makes a girl more interesting."

"Like *almost* spilling hot liquid all over them?" Jon teased. "I'd rather not have such intriguing surprises."

"Sorry about that," I said. "Totally unintentional."

"If you say so," Jon said, grinning for the first time during our conversation.

"Katelyn," Jon continued. "I'm not good at playing games and that's what it feels like with Joannie sometimes. I can't tell what she really wants, or what she's really up to. That's not to say that Joannie isn't a lot of fun. She's got a great sense of humor and she's smart and I think she'll be a good asset to the FF Club."

"I don't know Joannie all that well," I said, thinking to myself, *Everybody keeps telling me how wonderful Joannie is, so why don't I want to get to know her better?*

139

"I keep hoping that you and some of the other girls will get to know her better and have a positive influence on her."

Change her into someone you want as a girlfriend? I thought. That's not exactly what I had in mind!

"I hope I can get to know Joannie better," I said, although I'm sure that came off very half-heartedly. "I'm not sure, though, how much one person can help change another person. That's something I think only God can do."

"And that's probably what Joannie needs most—a better relationship with God. Add her to your prayer list."

Add her to my prayer list? I've got to be honest, dear Journal, that thought had *not* crossed my mind. Pray for Joannie? How? What for? That she might become Jon's girlfriend?

Jon answered the question for me, "Pray that she will want to know God in a deeper way."

I can pray for that. After all, that's something everybody needs. Katelyn Anna Louise Weber, included.

"OK, Jon," I said, "I will."

"And promise me you won't go to Mexico Pete's without me?" he added, with a big Jon Weaver grin.

"It's a deal," I said, grinning back.

"Want to go on a hay ride with me?" he then said, still grinning.

"Sure, why not?" I said, very lightheartedly. "How about a week from Saturday night?"

"I hear there's going to be a full moon," Jon said, still very much teasing me as he rinsed out his cup and left it in the sink.

"And a great one-act play starring The Weave in the role of Grandpa Stone," I added.

"Should be an incredible night," Jon said . . . grinning all the way to the front door.

"An amazing theatrical debut." I grinned back, holding the door open while he threw his wool scarf around his neck in true swashbuckler style.

"See you tomorrow," Jon said, with a final wink.

Since last night, I've thought back over what Jon said at least a dozen times. One thing really bothers me, dear Journal. Jon made a big point of our being honest with each other, and I feel guilty about that. The truth of the matter is, I *haven't* been honest with Jon lately, and especially tonight, about the way that I feel about him. He's more than "just a friend" to me, and I need to tell him that. If he laughs at me or pulls back, I guess I'll just have to accept that. But I've got to find a way to talk to him and see if maybe, just maybe, Jon is feeling the same way I am.

Chapter Fourteen

A Big Grand Weekend

I've just had two really big days, dear Journal. Friday night was the "big game"—our first of two encounters with our main rival, East Valley High. And we won, 17 to 14! Our team is really doing great this year. I think they're three and one so far.

We all went as a group to the game and sat together as a group, and then after the game, we went to Tony's as a group. Joannie and Smith and Kent were with us, along with two other kids who had said they'd still want to be part of the FF Club, regardless of whether we were an official school club or not: a guy named Hank and a girl named Kris. They are both really neat kids. Kris has just started to attend Faith Community Fellowship so she's in youth group, too. And Hank is in algebra with Libby and me. He's a neat guy and I can tell he's a Christian.

We had our own cheering section, or at least it felt that way. Julio would be a great cheerleader, except, of course, that all of the cheerleaders at Collinsville High are girls. If they ever add guy yell-leaders, Julio would be a shoo-in. He's got tons of enthusiasm. He was hoarse by the time the night was over.

Saturday was the big Grand Opening of Aunt Beverly's new store. Aunt Beverly asked a friend of hers, Bill George, to be in charge at The Wonderful Life Shop for the day. He used to have a shop a little like Aunt Beverly's in Benton (at least that's what Aunt Beverly says. I can't imagine anybody having a shop just like hers). Then he closed his shop to go exclusively into interior design. Aunt Beverly said that he has given her great advice over the years—he's nearly Grandpa Stone's age, I think—and he has suggested to his clients that they buy at The Wonderful Life Shop. I used to find it very confusing when Aunt Beverly would talk about Bill George . . . for months, I thought she was talking about two different guys. I finally just started calling him "the man with two first names." Mr. George is where I ended up!

Anyway . . . I helped with the cookies and hot cider table at the grand opening of the store. Which was really exciting. I could hardly believe the store. I hadn't been there in a week, and it was just amazing to see what it looked like with all the shelves and racks filled, and all the final pieces of furniture and rugs in place.

Aunt Beverly and Colleen had put a big red ribbon and bow over the two front doors of the store and a tarp over the sign above the doors. The mayor came over—wearing his big official medallion around his neck—and the photographer from *The Collinsville Press* was there to take a picture as he and Miss Jones, the president of the Collinsville Chamber of Commerce, cut the ribbon, with Aunt Beverly and Colleen looking on. There was quite a group of us gathered out on the sidewalk—including Jon and Mr. Clark Weaver, Dad and Grandpa Stone, Kiersten and Mari, and even Mrs. Miller. Several other store owners were there, too. Julio brought his trumpet, at Aunt Beverly's request, to give a quick fanfare when the ribbon was cut. Smith had brought a drum to do a little drumroll. (He plays drums in the band.)

Dennis and Hank were up on top of the store to pull back the tarp as soon as the ribbon was cut and Julio let out the first trumpet blasts.

It only took thirty seconds to open the store, but it was a fun thirty seconds! Collins Classics is now open in Collinsville!

I love the name Aunt Beverly chose. Originally, they were thinking about calling the store Colleen's Classics, since Colleen is going to be the manager. But both Aunt Beverly and Colleen thought that sounded like a women's shop. Then it was going to be Collinsville Classics, but Dad said he thought that sounded like an antique car dealership. So . . . they ended up with Collins

Classics. On the sign, "Collins" is big, and the word "classics" is underneath it in smaller, spaced-out letters, like this:

C O L L I N S
c • l • a • s • s • i • c • s

I think the sign looks like the store itself! It's very classic inside. Lots of dark wood and three or four chairs that are red and green plaid. The curtains over the dressing room areas are a combination of khaki and plaid (khaki on the top and plaid on the bottom two thirds of each curtain) and the light fixtures are old brass. Aunt Beverly found two big old hutches that she's using to display sweaters and accessories.

The pictures of the guys around the room look great. Originally, they were going to be big over-sized poster photos, but then Mr. Clark Weaver took such classic shots that Aunt Beverly decided to frame them in neat antique wooden frames that are sixteen by twenty inches. I helped her pick out several of the frames at the Antique Mart last week. The photos are still in black and white, but the velvet mats in the frames are all in deep red, green, brown, and other colors Aunt Beverly calls "hunt-scene colors." I think Jon's picture is the best of the twelve on display, but then again, I'm probably prejudiced.

While I was passing out hot cider and cookies, I had a chance to tell Mr. Clark Weaver that I thought he had done a great job with the photographs. (I figured if Joannie can play this little game, I can play it better! Oops—I'm not supposed to be into game playing, am I?) Anyway, Mr. Clark Weaver surprised me by saying, "I'd like to take some shots of you sometime, Katelyn. Especially while the trees are still so beautiful. How about it? Maybe Sunday afternoon, if the sun is out?"

"Sure," I said. "I'd be flattered."

"Actually," he whispered, "I think a photograph of you would be a great Christmas gift for your aunt."

"I agree," I whispered back, and added with a big tease in my voice, "but do you get to give it to her or do I?"

"Either way," laughed Mr. Clark Weaver. "Let's see what we can come up with." So, we set a time and he suggested that I plan to wear two or three different outfits. And we met earlier this afternoon at the park for a photo session . . . but more on that later.

The grand opening was a big success. Everyone who came in the store loved it, and I think Colleen sold quite a bit of merchandise. Even Dad and Grandpa Stone bought two sweaters each, and I think Dad also got a new belt. I heard Colleen talking with Aunt Beverly at the end of the day and she seemed very excited.

On Saturday night, we had our dress rehearsal and it went great. Trish is a fabulous Emily Pearson, and Julio was perfect in his role of trying to get her to take a drink from his flask. We had to look long and hard for a flask. Nobody drinks! Which is good . . . but difficult when it comes to flask finding! Kimber had found some neat old jackets for Julio and Kent to wear. Dennis is just going to wear a denim shirt and Jon only has to add an "ascot" to his outfit. Ford's only costume is going to be a hat and a pencil behind his ear.

This is going to be fun. Over cake, we compared notes, and everything seems to be in place. We've got the hay wagon all arranged, and the flyers for publicity have already gone out—thanks to Ford and Trish. Kimber has talked with pastors Bert and Sharyn again, and Libby and Julio have arranged for the marshmallows and roasting sticks. Ford, Smith, and Pastor Sharyn are bringing their guitars and have talked over the music. Jon got a roll of tickets to sell. I'm responsible for the lights and table and chairs we need for the play—Grandpa Stone is helping me with that, providing a portable generator and lights, and Aunt Beverly has a little table and two old-fashioned chairs I can use.

So I think all things are in order. We're going to start selling tickets on Monday at lunch. Trish surprised me by asking Jon, "Are you one hundred percent *sure* everything is really nailed down with Joannie's uncle?"

"Yes, finally," he said, sounding a little exasperated. "I went out and talked with him myself, and I'm going to go back out on Wednesday and make sure everything is squared away one more time."

"Was there a problem?" I asked.

"Nothing that couldn't be resolved with some honest, straightforward communication," Jon said, and went over to help himself to another piece of Mrs. Miller's scrumptious carrot cake. (I love the cream cheese frosting she made!)

"What happened?" I asked Trish on the side.

"It seems that Joannie got a little out of sorts when she realized she wasn't in your play," Trish said, and added with a little *hmff* to her voice, "I think she wanted my part."

"Is she still going on the hay ride?" I asked.

"I think so," Trish said. "For a while there, she was saying things like, 'I'm not sure my uncle is going to do this now'—making it sound like an excuse since we weren't an official school club. It was plain as day that she was just upset that she wasn't in the play."

"So what happened?" I asked.

"On Thursday after school, Jon and Dennis drove out there and talked to her uncle themselves. He was thrilled we wanted to come. Apparently he likes renting out his rig and does this for extra money each fall. He said he'd like to get to the place where he could book two or three hay rides every weekend for about seven or eight weeks each fall. He didn't have anything for next Saturday night so he was glad! He gave Jon a good price and showed him the campfire area, and he even made a suggestion to Jon that we hadn't thought of."

"What was it?" I asked.

"Actually, I think everybody should probably hear this," Trish said. So we called everybody to attention and Trish said that Joannie's uncle had suggested that we *start* the hay ride at the Emily Pearson park next to the high school. That would give us nearly an extra hour of ride, by the time we got loaded and went through the city streets and out on West Peter's Road to his farm, which is about ten miles out of Collinsville. We all agreed that was a great idea, and Jon said he'd call Mr. Field the next day to tell him that we were taking him up on his idea.

"We haven't t-t-talked about it," said Libby, "but is there a limit to the number of people we can have on the hay ride?"

"Mr. Field said he could pull two wagons with his tractor," said Jon. "Each wagon can hold up to thirty kids. He also said that if we wanted, he could make two runs." We talked about that a bit but decided that sixty kids would be more than sufficient for a hay ride. In fact, I'm not quite sure how we'd handle that many. But, I guess we'll just have to see who buys tickets. We did decide to sell the tickets for three dollars each. "It's as good as a movie," Ford pointed out, "and twice as long. Plus, they get refreshments."

Libby pointed out that there's something kind of nice about having a sell-out, and we agreed. As everybody left, Jon asked me very directly, "Do you want me to stop by and pick you up on Saturday so we can walk up to Emily's garden together?"

"Sure," I said. "That would be great."

"After all," he added, "it *is* where we first met."

"I remember," I said. I think it's neat that Jon remembered, too.

After church and lunch on Sunday, I spent about two hours with Mr. Clark Weaver—and Jon, too—taking photographs. Jon brought along his camera. I think they were having some kind of competition about who could take the best photographs of me. Anyway, they each took two rolls at the park and then I changed clothes and they took some of me on our front porch, and then of me looking out my bedroom window through the trees. I'm especially eager to see how those turn out! Both Jon and his dad actually climbed the tree to get the shots they wanted. At one point, Jon nearly fell out! It was fun playing model. Photographs could be what I give as Christmas gifts to Dad and Grandpa Stone and Gramma Weber, in addition to Aunt Beverly!

On to the week ahead! It's mostly routine until Saturday. I can hardly wait for our hay ride!

Chapter Fifteen

The Emily Pearson Memorial Hay Ride

Sunday
3 P.M.

*L*ast night was one of the best nights of my entire life! I hardly know where to begin. I probably should tell you about the week at school, but nothing major happened. It was pretty much routine as normal. I went to the second student council meeting and asked that I be allowed to bring up the subject of prayer in school clubs at the next meeting. I got an *A* on my history test and a *B* on my French test.

By Thursday at noon we had sold all sixty tickets to the hay ride! About a dozen kids asked us on Friday to buy tickets. I had mixed feelings about telling them that the event was sold out. On the one hand, I was sorry they couldn't go. On the other hand, I was glad it was a sell-out and that so many kids wanted to attend an FF Club event. Dennis said that many kids don't buy tickets to some of the official school club events.

Saturday was a perfect day for a hay ride. The trees are still pretty and the day was cool, but no wind. Saturday night, on the other hand, was clear and c-o-l-d. Time for heavy jackets and crocheted wool hats and scarves. A perfect fall night with a full moon.

Jon came by for me at about quarter to seven. Even though I knew it wasn't a date, it sort of felt like one. Kiersten had gone over to Mari's house. She and Mari were going to go with Dennis and Kimber, and then Kiersten was spending the night with Mari after the hay ride. So Jon and I walked alone to the school. He was in one of the best moods I've ever seen him in—teasing and grinning nonstop.

Mr. Field was there just as he had promised, and at seven o'clock, we all piled on the hay wagons. Jon counted everybody as they got on the wagons and sure enough, we had exactly sixty people. He helped me up and then climbed up and plopped down beside me. And at precisely seven-fifteen, we took off, rumbling rather clappity-clap style around the school and out to West Peter's Road. We probably weren't doing more than ten or fifteen miles an hour.

I've got to tell you—Joannie wasn't amused. Jon helped Joannie up onto the second wagon and I think she thought Jon was going to climb into that wagon to sit with her. Instead, we got into the first wagon. I like to think she *didn't* glare at me, but she didn't really smile at me, either.

For the first few minutes of the hay ride, everybody was so busy talking and joking around that it sounded like we were a hive of bees. And then Ford and Smith got out their guitars and we started to sing—lots of fun old kid songs, like "Old MacDonald Had a Farm" and "Skip to My Lou."

We made it out to the farm about eight o'clock. I wasn't watching the time very closely. After about fifteen minutes of driving through the fields, we came to the campfire location. Mr. Field's wife and children (junior high kids, I'd guess) had built the campfire and it was roaring when we showed up. Dad was there, too, with the generator and all the "set" arranged just as I had drawn out for him.

We got all the marshmallows distributed—and also some graham crackers and chocolate squares so we could make S'mores, too. But the fire was too high for good marshmallow roasting, so we decided to start with our skit.

It turned out great. A little more like a melodrama than I had thought it should be, perhaps, but it was perfect for the night. At first, some of the kids laughed as Julio tried to get Trish—that is, Emily Pearson—to take a drink. But after a couple more minutes, everybody got very serious. When the play was over, there were a few seconds of absolute silence—so quiet you could have heard a pin drop, except of course, that we were out in the middle of a farm—and then everybody applauded and cheered. Pastor Bert took over at that point and explained to everybody that the hay ride had been named the Emily Pearson Memorial Hay Ride in honor of Emily. He brought up one of my favorite scriptures in the Bible—Romans 8:28, "All things work together for good to those who love God."

Bert said, "You may not see how that verse fits in with what happened to Emily—but just stop to think for a minute. Emily went to be with the Lord because she knew Jesus Christ as her Savior, and most of the other people in that story had their lives changed, and here we are, lots of years later, still remembering her and her witness. Her life will continue to make a difference for good if just one person decides tonight never to ask another person to drink—or do anything they believe is wrong—against their will."

And then Pastor Sharyn took over and said just a few words, something to the effect that God is in the business of changing the bad parts of our lives into good parts. That's what the word "redemption" means, she explained. She said that Jesus died on the Cross so we could have meaning and purpose in life, and know that we are going to live with God forever, and that when a person makes a decision for Christ, it means that all things *do* work together for an ultimate good. At the end, Pastor Bert said that if any of the kids wanted to know more about Christ, he would be happy to talk to them. And we closed by singing "Amazing Grace." It was really neat.

And then it was time to roast marshmallows and sing some songs around the campfire. Joannie tried twice to get close to Jon, but each time, he managed to move away from her and come stand by me. Finally, she seemed to zero in on Hank. *Now there's an idea!* I thought.

We left the farm about ten o'clock, I think. Anyway, we got back to the school right at eleven o'clock—pretty much singing all the way. As the evening went on, the songs seemed to get mellower and mellower. A few of the couples who were considering this hay ride a "date" snuck a few kisses, but nobody did anything that was really embarrassing.

As the wagons unloaded, Jon and I made sure that everybody had a ride or way home. He also paid Mr. Field the second half of his fee. (He had paid the first half as a deposit.) In all, we cleared about seventy dollars on this event. Not bad, for something that seemed like total fun.

After the wagon pulled away, Jon surprised me by saying, "Let's pop in here for a minute." And he took my hand and pulled me toward the little garden where Emily's plaque and fountain are located.

Once there, Jon pulled off his cap and said, very

seriously, "Thanks, Emily, for the way you lived your life. I hope you know there in heaven that tonight was for you."

We stood there for a few minutes of silence and then I said, "I hope that nobody who went on the hay ride tonight ever tries to get anybody to drink when they don't want to."

And then after a few more seconds, we left. Jon never did quit holding my hand. It seemed so natural that I really didn't notice it until we had started walking home.

Jon was pretty quiet on the way home. He said that he thought this was the best FF Club party we had ever had, and that he didn't know what we'd end up doing with the money we raised, but he just knew that whatever it was that we decided to do, it would be good. I couldn't agree more.

When we were just a couple of houses away from home, I got up my courage and said, "Jon, you said something last week about our being honest with each other, and I think there's something I need to tell you—that is, if we're going to be *really* honest with each other."

"What is it?" Jon said.

"I don't quite know how to say this, and I hope you won't laugh at me," I said. I suddenly felt very nervous.

"Just say it, Katelyn," he said. "Whatever it is, it will be OK. We're friends."

"That's just the point," I said. "I think I'm starting to like you, Jon Weaver, as more than 'just a friend.'"

"Really?" said Jon. "That's a relief." He gave a big sigh.

"A relief?" I asked.

"Yeah," he said. "I was really starting to like you, too, as more than just a friend, but I didn't know how you'd feel about that."

"I feel pretty good, actually," I said, squeezing his hand a little and really feeling for the first time how good it was to have my hand in his.

"Good enough for me to kiss you good night, Miss Katelyn Anna Louise Weber?" he asked as he stopped outside the gate in front of our house.

"Yeah," I said. But before I could say more, Jon Weaver leaned over and kissed me! I felt like a little bit of electricity went all through me. He must have felt it, too, because after he kissed me, he said, "Wow. I've never had a friend quite like this!"

We both laughed and then he kissed me again—this time a little harder and longer. Dear Journal, it was *wonderful*. I don't think I've ever been more happy than I was right in that moment.

"Good night, Weave," I said.

"A very good night," he said, with that typical Jon Weaver grin. "See you tomorrow at church."

I raced upstairs and gave Dad a big hug in the hall. He said, "You sure look happy."

"I am!" I said.

"The hay ride was a big success then?" he asked. "I got the set arranged the way you wanted?"

"Exactly," I said. "It couldn't have been better."

"You like hay rides, I take it," Dad said with a smile. I probably should have told Dad about Jon kissing me, but I didn't want to tell anybody right then. I just said, "I *love* hay rides."

After I got ready for bed, I sat by the window for a little bit. I couldn't see the moon from there but I could see the moonlight hitting the trees. *Thanks, God, that I'm fifteen and in Collinsville. Thanks for all my friends and for all the fun I had tonight. And thanks, God, for letting Jon be my friend . . . and my boyfriend.*

I'm sure He understood how grateful I really am.

And now it looks like it's time to start yet another journal. I can hardly wait to see what I'll have to write in it—

What will it be like to have a real boyfriend . . . and for that boyfriend to be Jon Weaver?

Will Aunt Beverly and Mr. Clark Weaver get back together like they were before?

Will Collins Classics be the big success we all hope it will be?

Will I be able to make any difference in Collinsville High as sophomore class secretary?

Will I ever get a chance to talk to Libby about her relationship with Julio?

What *will* we decide to do with the money we made on the hay ride?

There's so much to think about—but for now, I've got to run. Jon is picking me up for youth group in about half an hour, and my hair is an absolute mess!

A very very happy Katelyn Weber!

The first three books in the Forever Friends series are available at your local Christian bookstore.

New Friends in New Places (Book One)
Since moving to Collinsville at the end of her freshman year, Katelyn Weber has decided three things—she hates Jon Weaver, she'll never make any friends, and she is happy eating lunch alone every day with her nose in a book. She soon discovers, however, that this isn't what God intends for her life. A surprising make-over, fellowship in the church youth group, and Jon's friendship prove to Katelyn that you never can tell just what God has in store.

Friends Make the Difference (Book Two)
Katelyn is amazed by all the new friends she's made, and what better way to stay friends than form a club? To serve the community and to make even more friends, Katelyn and the others decide to start the FF Club. Romance is in the air for Kimber and Dennis, and Jon gets a new look—one that turns Katelyn's head.

Summer of Choices (Book Three)
Katelyn and the other members of the FF Club do some amateur detecting to find out who's trying to sabotage the club's big Labor Day fundraiser. And when Trish, upset by her parents' problems and afraid that God doesn't care, runs away, her friends in the club try to show her their love and bring her back to God.